MW01001507

THE MAILBOX TREE

THE MAILBOX TREE

REBECCA LIM *and* KATE GORDON

WALKER BOOKS
AND SUBSIDIARIES

LONDON • BOSTON • SYDNEY • AUCKLAND

First published in 2024
by Walker Books Australia Pty Ltd
Gadigal and Wangal Country
Locked Bag 22, Newtown
NSW 2042 Australia
www.walkerbooks.com.au

Walker Books Australia acknowledges the Traditional Owners of the country
on which we work, the Gadigal and Wangal peoples of the Eora Nation,
and recognizes their continuing connection to the land, waters and culture.
We pay our respect to their Elders past and present.

 A catalogue record for this
book is available from the
National Library of Australia

ISBN: 978 1 760659 41 7

Typeset in 12pt Adobe Caslon Pro
Printed in China

This is a work of fiction. Names, characters, places and incidents are either the
product of the author's imagination or, if real, are used fictitiously. All statements,
activities, stunts, descriptions, information and material of any other kind contained
herein are included for entertainment purposes only and should not be relied on
for accuracy or replicated as they may result in injury.

10 9 8 7 6 5 4 3 2 1

*To my children, my terranauts – Oscar, Leni, and Yve –
you carry all my great love and hope for you, and the
world we live in, into the future. –* R.L.

*This one is for my Amelie. I see the past and future in
your eyes. I promise to spend the rest of my days
making your future a sweet one. –* K.G.

Nyx

"You've got to understand, Nyxie," Dad said, his voice the usual strange mix of urgent and hopeless, "when the floods come, and they're gonna come, someday soon, *home* will be gone. In my lifetime we've lost Tranmere, Lauderdale, Seven Mile Beach. The floodgates and seawalls we've built over the years have only made things worse. The old airport's been under water for almost a decade and Battery Point and Taroona are just memories kicking around in the heads of some really old people now."

Usually, I tune out, because Dad rattles off his *List of Doom* – that's what I call it – all the time, but there's something about the way he's speaking today that's scaring me.

"It's all changed beyond belief – even in my lifetime. Tasmania isn't one island now – it's at least *two*. Please, love, you're a smart kid. We *have* to leave. We are leaving. You can fight me all you want – but you can't fight the future."

There it is. Proof. He thinks I haven't heard him setting things up, arranging things, he's been too scared to tell me. But he's done it. Dad's finally done it.

Everything I'm chewing turns to dust in my mouth and I push away from the table so hard I set the battered orange pendant light over our kitchen table swinging. "I'm going outside," I say curtly and back it up by slamming out the back door so hard the swollen weatherboards of the lean-to back section of our house all shake at once.

Dad's mad with his talk about the flood. Tasmania's, lutruwita's, a dust bowl, only the edges of which are drowning. The rest of it is hot and gusty, gritty and dry, most of the ancient forests gone, along with regular snow fall, which I've only ever seen pictures of. Fire's always been a bigger problem than water. Always, as far as I can remember. That, and the lack of fresh food, which is so expensive no one around here eats anything but cryo – if they're rich – or rehydro, if they're not. The seas around us have turned so acidic that wild oysters, mussels and clams are mostly gone, crabs and lobsters, too.

Whole flocks of birds and bats have fallen out of the sky, at once. Bushfire season is all year round now, and we're all living like we're holding our breath, collectively, all the time because there's no water to put it out with. Just chemicals, which only make our land and our rivers worse after the rotas leave, first dumping their giant loads of dry powder over the fire front and peeling away through the choking air like giant bees, which are pretty much all gone as well.

"Nature's turned her back on us," my teacher told my class sadly, one of the few times we were all together in the one place, "because we turned away from her first."

I burst into a run – across our hot and dusty backyard full of dead things and through the sagging gate in the falling down wooden fence; up through the guts of a network of old cobblestoned alleys filled with falling down old houses just like mine, two hundred, almost three hundred years old. People are used to seeing me bolt through the back streets of West Hobart, nipaluna, in the twilight; so no one calls out, no one tries to stop me. It's too hot to care, my hair's already stuck fast to my face and neck, so that I can't really see properly to run.

I can't believe Dad's ranting about the flood again,

the flood to end all floods, he calls it, that's going to wipe out everything I've ever known; my whole entire life.

Unless we move first.

As far as I'm concerned, my dad's the flood. I know he's fallen in love with some lady he's met in a chat room for singles that he goes to in his head, where I can't hear what's happening or being said, or promised. I don't hear the words he's using, but I hear him laugh out loud – bursts of silence punctuated by loud laughter, the kind of real laughter I used to hear before Mom got sick and died – and I know he's found someone on the Northland; which is what we call the land mass to the north, funnily enough. 'Australia' takes too long to say, and this was palawa country before it was ever even Australia, everyone knows that, so we don't say it so much these days. And we don't really feel part of it anymore, on our island everyone stopped calling it *The Apple Isle* a long time ago because they're all gone, the apples. There's no water for growing apples, or any other kind of fruit for that matter.

I reach the old sports ground that once used to be green, people say; a great green oval where people came together to do things during the day, whenever they felt

4

like it. No one can be bothered doing things in groups now while the sun's out. It's too horrible, and you could catch something because "we are all seething hotbeds", my teacher often says wisely, "of killer germs and disease. Remember the pandemic that wiped out millions? And the ones after that?"

I only go to school now when it's unavoidable and there's a detention involved if you don't show up, because I can downlink the rest. Everything not just at your fingertips, but behind your eyes, speaking direct into your head, any time you want it. Some people never go outside anymore. They think it's too dangerous.

I reach the tree. The great towering pine that is the only surviving bit of green out here, only because it's at least forty yards tall, with thick, twisted roots that go deep into the ground. People care enough about it to come out and water it sometimes, talk to it, the way I'm doing now with my words, and my tears. Otherwise, the world is dust.

The rough bark of the lower branches scratches up my palms and fingers but I keep climbing. Up and up to the branch that has become my own – that overlooks the dust bowl of the old sports oval – with the small, hollow knot at waist height, a bit bigger than my closed fist. I used to be scared that snakes would come out of there, but no snake has been seen in West Hobart since 2055. It's been too hot, even for snakes. Maybe they'd all just lain down in their holes, one day, and died.

There's no breeze tonight, but the air is a little cooler because it's filtering through the branches of the tree that keeps on going, keeps on growing, against all sense and reason.

I dig a scrap of torn paper out of the pocket of my shorts and grip the stub of my pencil tight. My handwriting is terrible because just about no one uses paper any more to write with. Paper is hard to come by. This bit is off the back of an old book going spotty and yellow in my mom's last box of things that I keep in my bedroom.

It's faster now to just send words out through one of the little rooms in your head and Dad's embraced the chatting in a big way because we're dying out here, he says. We're marooned and getting more and more cut off as more people leave and nothing is made, nothing is grown, nothing is renewed. When the systems are down, and the chat rooms are closed to him, Dad's moods are blacker than black. "We might as well be dead and buried already!" I hear him roar through the walls of my bedroom as he bangs and crashes around in his own space. "What is the point?"

But I hate those rooms. I hate that people can knock on the doors of the rooms in your head, day or night, even when you have an invisible sign up that says: *Not talking* or *No callers* or *Not welcome*. The signs are *always* up in my head. But it doesn't stop people trying to sell me things or cross my very clear boundaries, 24/7/365. The calls I hate the most are the ones from strangers asking if they can see my legs, or my hands. It's creepy.

Using my hot, sticky thigh as a table, I write:

Until I fill up one whole side of the paper and have to turn over the scrap. There is a page number in a lower corner on the other side and not enough room to write all that again and, anyway, I'm crying so hard I can barely see, so I write in big screaming letters:

I REFUSE TO MOVE. I LOVE IT HERE.

I underline: **LOVE IT HERE**.

Home might be dying, and drier than the bone of a long dead animal, but it's still home. I don't want another one.

Then I shove the scrap into the hand-sized knot in the tree and hope that the wind carries my words away, like it always does.

Usually, I feel better as soon as the words pass out of my brain, into my fingers, onto the paper. But this time, the rage is still there and I bury my face in my crossed arms and howl so loud that I get feedback. All the sensors and the ingestibles inside my body sending the reverb from my own howling back into my ears, from the inside.

Bea

My mother peers at me over her half-moon glasses. She knows. She always knows. She always sees the heart of me.

She always sees my sadness.

And this sadness is big, and deep, and colored the vivid green of the leaves of my pine tree.

She knows that, inside, I am tearing, rending, falling apart.

My father has no idea.

"Excellent, if I do say myself," he grins at us, through a mouthful of ratatouille – not the traditional kind, with eggplant and zucchini. My dad's ratatouille is a study in found objects. This version has peas and sweet potato. Another bowl of it might contain kale and sultanas.

"Bea?"

Mom taps her fingernails on the table. Today, they

9

are decorated with pink and purple stickers. Her best friend, Ali, has gone into business selling them.

Ali had asked me if I wanted some – they came in kid versions, too, she said, with unicorns and flamingos on.

I told her I couldn't wear nail stickers, when I was climbing pine trees all the time.

"It won't be so different," Mom says now.

"What are you talking about?" Dad looks from one to the other of us, completely bemused.

"It will be," I mutter. "It won't be here. It won't be *home*."

"But there's so much you don't like about *here*," Mom reminds me. I dart a sidelong glance at Dad. I never like talking about this stuff – the bullying stuff – in front of him. Dad was bullied as a kid, too, and he always tells me that I just have to ignore the other girls and get on with things. He says that's what worked for him. He says they'll get bored of it, in time.

But they haven't bored of it, yet. It's been five years and they haven't bored of it.

It was like they marked me out, on our first day of school – I was 'different'. I lived up the hill in West Hobart. My parents were 'crunchy'. They were 'nerds', too. Before I started school, I never realized there was anything wrong with binge-watching the *Lord of the Rings* movies, at least once every couple of months. I never knew that keeping bees and making your own honey and beeswax lunch wraps was weird.

Those girls let me know, in no uncertain terms, that the life I lived – the person I was – was, *is*, freakish.

My hand-me-down uniform and home-cut hair are pathetic. My glasses make me look like a frog. The fact that I have hearing loss and sometimes have to ask our teacher to repeat things … that was flipping *bizarre*.

I am bizarre.

I spend all day at school, feeling like I am the only person who's come there from another planet.

The only place I feel really at home is *here*. In this house. That Dad is now asking me to leave. In two months' time.

Why can't Dad see that? A new school in a new place won't make a difference. I'd been marked out as weird here. Why would it be any different at a new school? There are mean girls everywhere and they will always think I'm a freak.

But there is only one *here*. Only one home. Only one

special tree that I can whisper my problems to. The sky I see above me, from my perch on my branch, is *my* sky. The currawongs and rosellas who share the tree are my *friends*.

And besides, we are *lucky* to live here. Tasmania is one of the safest, cleanest, most stable places on Earth. Why would we want to give this up to live on the mainland, with its crowds and its pollution and its *danger*?

Why would we want to give up our place? Our home?

My heartland.

I can't lose this place. I can't. It is all I have.

"I don't want to go," I mumble, trying hard to blink away the tears. Only Mom hears me.

"Honey–"

"No." I shake my head and shrug off Mom's arm. "Don't. I have to ... I'm just going out, for a while."

"Be home for dinner," Mom calls out after me while Dad continues to tuck into his lunch, oblivious of my pain. "We're having tempeh salad!"

I wave goodbye, over my shoulder, and run to my tree. It stands, at least twenty-five yards high, overlooking the football oval near my house.

"Hello, friend!" I call out to it, feeling the weight

immediately lifting from my shoulders.

I scale the trunk in minutes – my muscles recognizing every knot and twig and foothold automatically – and I take a seat on my favorite branch. Right by that weird knot in the trunk that's just a bit larger than my fist.

When I settle, I take a moment to center and calm myself. I breathe in the scent of eucalyptus and *clean* that is like nowhere else on Earth.

And then I do what I often do, up in these branches.

I talk to the tree.

Sometimes, I do it out loud. But I know Mom will be watching me, out the back windows of our house. She might even have sneaked, already, to the place she considered her 'secret' hiding spot, behind the wattle tree somewhere below me, just to make sure I am all right.

She thinks I don't know. But I always knew. She's my mom. I can sense her, even if I can't always see her.

And when she follows me – to watch and make sure I'm okay (because I'm 'her baby and her heart') – I talk to the tree in my *other* way.

I pull out the battered *Neverending Story* notebook I keep in my top pocket and slip my pencil from its covers.

And I begin to write:

I can't leave this place. I can't. This whole island would have to disappear before I willingly leave it. They can't make me go. It will ruin everything.

Then I rip the page out of my notebook and shove the scrap into the knot in the tree and hope that the wind carries my words away, like it always does.

Except that there's a bit of scrunched-up paper already in there.

I quickly withdraw my fist that's bunched around my note, as if I've just been bitten by a snake.

Without realizing what I'm doing, I drop my note and let it blow away on the wind, reaching into the knot for the scrunched-up scrap.

It's been torn out of an actual printed book – *sacrilege!* – and it says on one side:

Feeling cold prickles all up and down my arms, I smooth the scrap of paper out and see that across the printed text on the other side of the torn page there is a message written in messy capitals:

I REFUSE TO MOVE. I <u>LOVE IT HERE</u>.

And that's when I start to shake. *I* could have written this note. Even the handwriting looks like mine.

On a clean page of my notebook I start a new note.

Dear ... you,

Writer of the note I found in my tree?

You are ...

Who are you?

It's weird that I'm writing to you, isn't it?

Your note wasn't here yesterday. I know, because I was here yesterday.

Are you all right?

I look again at the scrap of paper in my hand. They could be my words, on that piece of paper. But they're not mine. They belong to someone else. *Who?* I add more of my own.

I'm not all right. I don't know who I'm saying this to, but the words pour out on the page.

It can't hurt to be writing back to you like this, if you'll promise not to tell. I don't even know who I'm asking to promise. Perhaps I'm only writing to our tree.

Our Mailbox Tree.

But ...

You said those things, about hating him and about refusing to move and it could have been me.

That's me.

Because my dad wants to move away from here very soon and I should want to, too, because school is horrible, the girls are horrible, and maybe school would not be horrible, elsewhere, but ...

Maybe it would be.

And, even so, school isn't everything, but this place ...

Is everything.

I'm sorry that this is all in such a mess. My thoughts are nothing solid. They are like paper in the wind, floating and swirling, and I'm sorry for that, but it's just how my brain is, right now. Because Dad wants to take me away from everything I've ever known and the one place – this place – where I've felt safe.

Dear you:

Please don't think I'm unforgivably weird.

Dear you:

I feel like I can tell you anything because right now you're …

I don't know what you are. Maybe you can tell me.

I'll keep resisting.

We're supposed to be leaving in two months, but I'll keep resisting.

Because I don't think I would survive the agony of leaving.

Write back.

Please.

Please tell me how to stop us moving because I'm out of ideas.

I'll look for your note tomorrow.

I'm about to tear the note out of my *Neverending Story* notebook but then I remember that whoever she is that wrote that note – I'm going to keep believing it's a she, a girl just like me – didn't have any paper. Because she was pouring out her anger onto the torn page of a real *book*.

Impulsively, I stuff my whole notebook into the knot in the tree. It's only the size of my palm and it was almost finished anyway.

She can have it. If it means she will write back.

Nyx

"Nyxie!" Dad roars, his face flushed red, all the blood vessels in his forehead and temples standing out. "Come here! Come here *now*! We're out of time."

But I pretend I don't hear him and race out of the house, the broken screen door with the holes all through the wire netting slamming behind me, my black hair flying out behind me like a flag.

How dare he? We never agreed to this.

I never said: *Yes, Dad. Organise the Movecorp for today.*

He can pack the movecrates himself. We've got nothing anyway. Electronic junk beyond salvaging, crappy biosynth furniture that's supposed to mould itself to your body for extra support and comfort but has been breaking down for years because it's too worn out to repair itself; has been struggling to repair itself for almost as long as we've had it. Maybe we bought it that way.

The only things I'd want to keep are the things in Mom's box – and all I'd have to do is throw the whole box into a movecrate. Move sorted. That's me, done.

Only, I don't want to move. And he can't make me. Someone will have to put me into deep cryo and carry me out of here in a porta-hyber. I'm not going willingly.

Dad's sprung it on me without consultation, or warning. And he can jam it.

Not going, not doing it! I scream out, lungs burning, legs pumping, to the dry dustbowl oval with its single living pine tree.

My tree. The one thing in this world that doesn't judge me and sees me how I really am.

I'm crying and scrambling up into its branches so fast the tips of my fingers start to bleed from all the little cuts and grazes.

I thrust my hand into the knot to find the note I left there yesterday so that I can rip it into pieces and throw it to the heavy breeze that's blowing dust and grit into my eyes.

But I stop short, drawing my hand back sharply at the touch of something cold.

Snake! My brain is screaming.

I look at the tips of my fingers and wonder if the blood on them is from the climb up here, or from a bite.

But the thing had felt hard. Ridged. Alien. Unsnakelike.

Despite the fear thrilling along all my nerves I slowly put my hand back into the knot in the tree and withdraw …

A book?

Is it though?

I study the thing in my hand. It's only slightly larger than my palm with a glossy cover. Just this weird-looking-maybe-book with a coil of thin metal running up its spine, to keep the handful of remaining pages together.

It's not like any book I've ever seen. It's got pictures of two real-looking people on the front cover, a boy facing a girl – Mom used to call them … photos? – and a name across the top that I'm not familiar with – 'The Neverending Story'.

I frown. Are the people in the photo … famous? Famous people don't do photos that don't move now. That's olden days stuff. Now, they send you vids, chats or interactives, straight into the space behind your eyes if you pay enough, or you've subscribed to their #official. Should I *know* them?

I feel around in the knot some more, but my note from yesterday isn't there anymore.

The book in my hand looks brand new, like something drone-dropped by mistake from on high, destined for someone else in the neighborhood but squirreled inside by the first person who finds it because, you know, *finders keepers*. That's the rule now. If you get there first and no one sees? It's yours.

Although pages have been torn out of the book. I can see that there are tiny shreds of torn paper in the coiled metal spine. Who would do this to a book? But then I realize that maybe it was made to be this way. And am amazed even more by how wasteful that seems.

I turn the book around and around in my hands, absorbing its shine. The newness and cleanness of it. Its complete and utter alien-ness. I sniff it, and it smells so new, not dried out, foxed and musty, the way Mom's old books smell. It's kind of neat. And useful. Like a memory room you'd keep inside your head – but sitting outside your body as a *thing*. Something concrete on which you can scrawl your thoughts that hasn't already had some other purpose. Like the page of the book I scrawled all over, yesterday.

I open the strange book's cover and actually feel dizzy when I see the words written in there that start:

Dear ... you,
Writer of the note I found in my tree?

It's *my* tree. I feel a surge of possessive anger. Nobody comes here but me. Nobody climbs it but me.

My eyes race down the first page then the next, taking in the scrambled words, but the meaning and our shared circumstances are clear. I wonder who she is – this girl, like me, who is being forced to move away against her will. Imagine – there are two of us in the same neighborhood! Being made to do what they don't want to by someone bigger who just doesn't get it.

I write hurriedly:

I'm out of ideas – Dad's organised the Movecorp for today. The living area is piled high with movecrates. It's actually happening. All our furniture's gone, packed up like it never was. It doesn't even feel like home anymore, just walls around a bunch of boxes.

He's met someone that isn't Mom and that's it – my old life is about to be a memory and my new one will be somewhere else. On the Northland.

He says it will be good for us but she's got kids. I think I'm going to hate them the same way they're gonna hate me.

If you get this, I might not be here tomorrow. You've got longer than I do. You're lucky.

I'm hoping you get a better result than me!

Good luck.

Nyx

I tear the piece of paper out of the book and start folding it, intending to put it back in the knot. But then I remember that she's given me this book – I'm keeping it, it's the most wondrous thing I've seen for a long time. Kind of old-fashioned, but utterly new at the same time. I frown, thinking how I've brought nothing to give her. But then I remember the one thing I have on me that she might be able to use, and rip the tired old biosynth timekeeper I'm wearing around my wrist off my skin.

It shrinks and deflates immediately, losing shape as soon as it's away from the warmth of my body. I shove it into my folded note, wrapping it tightly into the folds of paper.

I hope she knows that it means:

Thank you.

Crying again, I climb slowly back down my tree – what had she called it? *Mailbox Tree* – the strange book with the glossy cover clenched between my teeth, delicately, so that I don't mark it.

Bea

At the edges of my school playground there are gum trees and pine trees, lined up like guards, protecting us from the world. Just over the fence, there is the main road and cars and people and all the terrifying things.

We are safe, inside the gates, behind the trees.

I love it and hate it, at the same time.

The people out there scare me. I watch enough movies and read enough books to know that not all people are good and some of the people who walk past every day might be dangerous. I like knowing there are the high gates and the tall trees and teachers patrolling, to make sure nobody gets in.

But sometimes I feel like I'm in a cage.

At home, I can run as far as my legs will take me. I am free. I am also safe, because I know that Mom can see, from our kitchen window, every part of our property. I know that, when I'm outside, she stands at the window with her cup of coffee and a book and keeps an eye on me.

She pretends she doesn't. Sometimes, she ducks down if I turn to face her. She thinks I'll be mad at her for 'helicoptering' but the truth is, I like it. I like feeling protected and free at the same time. It's like there's an invisible cord, connecting me to her and it stretches to the farthest reaches of the universe but it's strong enough to pull me back home, before I fall into the abyss.

At school, the cord is still there, but it's not as strong. Mom can't help me as quickly if I fall.

And neither can the teachers, because they have a hundred kids to watch out for, not just me, so I sometimes slip through the cracks.

I sometimes fall, not into the abyss, but at the feet of the girls who would push me there if they could.

Which is why I'm up a tree now.

It's not my tree at home, but it's still comforting.

I press my back into the bark and it feels like safety.

The girls are particularly vicious today. Not for any reason. Just because they can – same reason as every day.

Mom and the teachers and everyone say it's nothing I'm doing wrong, nothing wrong with me, that those girls are just mean to *everyone*. But it's not true. They're mean to me because I'm different from them, from everyone. And everyone knows it. I think differently. I talk differently. My brain is just wired differently from most people and I've always known it and they know it, too. They can smell it on me. I am *weird*.

They knew it on the first day of school, when nobody wanted to sit with me.

They know it every day, when I'm called on in class, and I don't know how to reply in the same sort of language they use, when I use words they call 'big' and 'complicated' and 'bizarre'. When they catch me talking to flowers, or the sky.

So much so that I try not to do it anymore. But they still catch me doing *things*. Things that seem normal to me, but to them are monumentally *strange*.

This morning, before school, I was sitting on the grass and just … pressing my hands into the dirt. I just liked the way it felt. I felt connected. *Safe*.

Victoria was the one who noticed, and she called out to Scarlet, who ran over with Marina.

And now I have dirt on my face and I am called 'Dirt Girl'.

And they didn't put dirt on my face. They're too clever for that. They know that the teachers would see that and they'd be put in Time Out.

No, instead of that, and very quietly, Victoria said to me, "Rub your face, Dirt Girl."

And I know, by now, that it's useless to refuse her. If I refuse her, it just gets worse.

So I rubbed my face.

And then Victoria smiled and whispered, so sweetly, "You're not allowed to wash your face until after school."

And then they walked off.

And I ran away, and climbed a tree and now there are tear tracks in the dirt but I can't wipe them away because it might wipe the dirt away, too, so now when I get down, they'll see the dirt and they'll see I've been crying.

They didn't push me into the abyss but I still feel like I'm falling.

I wiped my face with tissues and drink bottle water after school, so I'm clean(ish) when Mom meets me at the school gates. She kisses my head and ruffles my hair and says, "Good day, sweetheart?" and I should be bothered by all that affection – should be embarrassed – but I'm not because I'm with her and I'm safe now.

"Okay," I tell her. And then I change the subject. "I finished my homework already, so can I go outside when I get home?"

"After a shower and a snack," she tells me, same as she always does.

Mom is very big on snacks.

I showered yesterday, so I know it means she can see a bit of the dirt on my face still, but hopefully it's not enough to worry her. Just the normal level of dirt for a kid who likes climbing trees and pressing her hands into dirt.

"Deal," I tell her.

"Excellent." She kisses my head again. "I bought Oreos. Don't tell your dad. You can have one if you have some fruit as well."

"Can I take it up the tree?" I ask her. I add quickly, "I promise not to choke and if I do I'll do it noisily so you come and save me."

Her brow furrows for a really long time, as she considers my proposal (Mom has a thing about staying still while you're eating, so you don't swallow something the wrong way and *die*). Finally, she sighs.

"Did you have a bad day, sweetheart?" she asks, quietly.

Obviously, my deflection a couple of minutes ago hasn't worked. I have to try something different. Telling her the truth might be the only way she'll let me go straight to the tree.

"Yeah,' I say.

"Do you want to talk about it?'

I shake my head. "Not yet. I just need to … decompress."

She sighs again. Some days, my mom is just one big cacophony of sighs. But she nods finally and says, "Okay, when we get home, just grab your snack and you can go up. But no grapes. And shower after. You'll only end up getting dirty again while you're climbing."

I wrap her in my arms and she is warm and she is soft and she smells like vanilla and eucalyptus and she is *safe* and I love her the most of anything.

When we get home, I do as she says and I take an Oreo and a container of raspberries (the least choke-worthy fruit in the house), and run out to the tree. My tree.

And *climb*.

And it's like my soul exhaling.

And I tell myself I won't do it.

Because it's ridiculous to think that there will be something there.

Ridiculous.

But I can't help myself. I scoff the biscuit and fruit (making sure to chew in an ostentatious way, so that Mom can almost see it from the window), and when I'm done, I shove my hand in the knot in the tree.

After checking for snakes first, of course. I'm not an idiot.

At first I'm disappointed. There's nothing there. My notebook is gone.

But then I feel around some more, really poke fingers into all the spaces inside the knot, even though I'm terrified, and I feel a square of squishy paper. I draw it out, open it and … *something* falls out.

Some weird, flesh-colored *something* that looks a bit like a shriveled, dark tan-colored band, just slightly wider than one of my fingers.

What the …

I flatten it out and it starts to feel … warm. In my fingers. Like it's drawing the heat out of my body.

What is it? I stretch out the ends of it, draping it over one wrist and bright numbers suddenly flash up. I jump, and the thing almost falls to the ground, many feet below. I catch it before it can slip off my wrist completely. It's a watch! I think.

I shove it into a pocket of my jeans for safekeeping and open the square of torn notebook paper.

And my heart begins to thud even faster. If that's possible.

She wrote back! I feel a surge of joy.

But as I begin to read, my heart starts to deflate. She's moving? Leaving? *Today?* I frown at the unfamiliar word *Northland*. Does she mean the mainland? Or somewhere else? Somewhere even further? *North* is a pretty big place.

She may already be gone.

But she can't! She's my … friend? Is that too weird? Is it the strangest thing I've ever done, to consider some stranger who wrote me a note left in a hole in a tree…

A friend?

But she might be the closest thing I've ever had to one, or at least to someone who doesn't treat me like a pariah.

She can't already be gone.

I take out my pen and I begin scribbling, furiously, on the back of the paper she left me.

No! I begin. *Don't go! I need you!* And I shove my balled-up reply back into the knot and cry, for a long time.

Nyx

I'm still so shocked that my hands are shaking and my writing is all over the place.

It's been delayed, I write, and my letters are all sloppy like a little kid's.

The Movecorp couldn't take the boxes because the ship to the Northland <u>took out</u> the Tasman Bridge! The driver was drunk, or drugged on Pink Death, they think, and he drove the cargo ship straight through one span of it. Loads of people died, it's really sad, their self-drive Autos just drove straight off the two edges and fell into the water because even though the Autos in front knew to stop, the Autos behind just pushed the ones in front right over. People on boats in the water said it was like seeing toy Autos pile up and go over. Dozens of them.

None of the people in the Autos that fell could take control of them fast enough or get out because the doors wouldn't open. It's a 'national tragedy', people are calling it.

They are still searching for bodies. The ship's been quarantined in port until they can work out how it happened and who to blame for all the deaths, and the damage. We can't move until the whole mess is cleared up! Do you

I hesitate over my next words then write quickly. *want to meet up? To just talk?*

I feel like Bea would understand. She's in the same place I am. When Dad finally tracked me down to the Mailbox Tree and bawled for me to come down or he'd call the Citizens Police on me, I was puffy from crying and he'd snarled that the bridge had completely collapsed, and I'd got my way because there was no move in the foreseeable future. Not until they'd laid charges on the ship's captain, and the Movecorp, and anyone else they could squeeze money out of because Hobart was desperate for public funds, and the bridge disaster – they were calling it a *disaster* – was the 'cash cow' the city had been praying for. (I still wasn't sure what a cash cow was.

Wasn't a cow a kind of animal that used to roam around everywhere on things called 'farms'? What did cash have to do with it?) Not to mention all the families left behind from the people who'd gone over in the Autos. A lot of them would be destitute now and who was going to feed them? It would take weeks, maybe months, to unravel the mess.

"Just my luck!" Dad had shouted, standing at the bottom of the Mailbox Tree. "Just my bleeding luck when finally, something good was going to happen, Nyx, honestly. It's like we're cursed."

I think I held my breath until he finally stumped away home, still swearing and smashing his right fist into his left palm.

I'll be here from 6pm tomorrow, I write hurriedly. *When the sun's not so hot and I won't get sick from the radiation.*

I add: *Thank you for the book – the 'Neverending Story' book. I love it. I've never had so much real paper, clean paper, just to write on. I hope the biosynth band is behaving. It's not new, none of our stuff ever is, but it should still be able to do what you want it to. Just talk to it and tell it when you want to wake up, or record or* dial. It's old, but it still works okay, although it doesn't look like much.

Please come.

It's been so long since I could really talk to someone. And I feel like you would understand. I'd just like to see you – before we have to leave. Maybe we could still write to each other, or see each other, you know, chat or vid, when I get to the Northland? I'd love that. You don't know what it means, to know someone who's going through the exact same thing as me.

Then I fold the piece of miraculous, shiny-new, clean paper from the 'Neverending Story' book that Bea left me and I climb back down the tree.

Bea

I read the note that Nyx left me again, for the third time.

My heart is beating so fast, it feels like it belongs to a mouse. We had a class mouse, in Grade 4, and when we held it we were all astounded by how quickly its tiny heart beat, like it was terrified of some lurking predator. Our teacher said it had something to do with how fast its metabolism ran, and that scientists used to believe that having a fast metabolism meant an animal didn't live as long, which was why mice only live for a few years. Now they know that the reason mice don't live for as long is because of predators. If an animal has lots of predators, and is *expected* to be eaten at a young age, it makes sense that they grow and reproduce – and die – really quickly.

So, I guess, all of that ties together, somehow. Mice heartbeats are so fast it seems like they are always scared;

always running; always fearing predators. And it's not their fast heartbeat that makes them die young, really. It's the predators.

I don't know. It makes a kind of sense in my head.

Right now, my heart is beating like a mouse's: like there is a predator hunting *me*, and I hope that doesn't mean I'll die young. Probably all it means is that evolution is weird and so is life and if you need any more evidence of that, you only need to look at this note.

Quite apart from the fact that it appeared, by magic, in the hollow of the Mailbox Tree – I call my tree that now, all the time.

If you leave that aside, there's another – huger – reason why it's bizarre. Because Nyx just said that a big ship crashed into the Tasman Bridge!

But I watched the news last night, during tea, and that didn't happen. Nobody said anything about the Tasman Bridge. Daddy takes the Tasman Bridge to work every day, and he never said anything about there being a problem.

Or, at least, if a big ship did crash into the Tasman Bridge, it happened a very, very long time ago. I only know about it because my grandparents were on the bridge when the ship struck. They were far enough back in their car – or in Nyx's word their *Auto* – that they were safe, but close enough to see the cars going over into the water. Nyx was right though. It was the captain's fault because he was drunk, and the bridge collapse killed twelve people. It impacted Hobart hugely, because the two shores were cut off from each other for a long time, and people found it very hard to travel between them, to get to work, to school, even to hospital if they were really sick.

But all of this happened – *in 1975.*

I start shivering, I can't help it. Unless I missed something yesterday … Nyx is …

From 1975?

Which is … I can't even get my head around what that is. But something about it doesn't make sense.

Nyx keeps talking about this 'biosynth' band she left me in the Mailbox Tree – it just looks like a weird, shrivelled piece of tan-colored stuff, like a used Band-Aid, but a bit bigger, with no holes or markings. It's just smooth and slightly squishy. In her last note she said it can make calls and record stuff and make you wake up?

I pull the squishy, used Band-Aid thing out of my shirt pocket now and my heart is beating like a mouse's, and my brain feels all full of goo and none of it makes sense and none of it is possible and it can't be real.

I turn it over and over in my hands. It still looks, and makes me feel, really icky but …

Gingerly, I dangle it over the top of my wrist again and bend over it, gasping as I watch it somehow – *magically* – unwrinkle and flatten and grip me around the wrist, tight, so it almost feels as if it has become part of me.

It fits *perfectly*. Like it was made for me, except that it's a darker shade than my own skin and I realize that it was maybe made to blend in with *Nyx's* skin.

I shudder. It's all too freaky and I want to take it off, right away, I shake my wrist, trying to fling it off me, off the tree, so that it will fall down to the ground, where it can turn into compost, along with the fallen leaves and possum poo, but … if I let it fall, then I'll never know.

And I have to know.

I slowly raise my wrist to my lips and I say, "Hello?" Squeezing my eyes shut in terror at what I might hear back. Will Nyx be there?

But there's no noise, not even a crackle. The band stays smooth and silent. It's not a phone then. I poke at the top of it and numbers suddenly flash up again, a bright aqua color – 5.37 – and I almost fall off the branch I am sitting on in panic before I exhale. It's just a watch. A freaky looking watch, but it's telling me the same time as my regular watch on my other wrist and I feel suddenly happy that Nyx has given me her own watch! Just because I left her half a used notebook to keep. Maybe she does want to be friends, because friends do that, give each other stuff, and that's amazing.

I flatten out Nyx's note again and feel goosebumps.

If her note is right – she's going to meet me here at 6pm! That's only about 20 minutes away.

My heart feels enormous in my chest. I'm beyond excited at the thought of actually meeting Nyx, but I'm also feeling a bit nervous. I feel like we already sort of know each other through our letters.

But what if she only likes me on paper? What if she doesn't like who I *really* am? I mean, I don't really have friends, in real life. Nobody else seems to like me. They think I'm a freak and a weirdo and a loser. Why should I expect that Nyx would be any different? But …

What if she is?

What if she's the friend I've always been destined to make? The one person who understands me that isn't my mom. The one person, besides Mom, who sees me as I really am and *likes* me?

I know it's a lot of pressure to put on one person, and it's not really fair, considering we haven't even really met yet, but this feels momentous. And important.

And I feel like the entire inside of my body, beneath my skin, is full of butterflies and biting ants and they are at war with each other. Part of me wants to run, because then the ants will stop biting, but the butterflies will go away, too, if I do that. And I like their excited fluttering.

So, I wait.

I wait and I scan the ground below me, seeking out any sign of life. I wait for ten minutes, then – my heart in my chest – I wait as the strange new watch on my wrist shows me that twenty minutes have passed. It's 6pm. And she hasn't come.

My heart deflating bit by bit, I wait as it becomes thirty minutes, then forty. When it becomes fifty, I – finally, miserably – climb down from the Mailbox Tree.

She didn't come.

She didn't come because I am a freak and she realized it. She realized I'm a loser and she decided it would be better if she never met me at all. Or, she did come and she saw me, up here, and she *saw* how much of a loser I am.

I tell myself, either way, it's probably for the best that we never met. If this is as bad as it gets, this is bad enough. But …

One tiny, hopeful butterfly has stayed on, inside me. I feel it flapping its wings.

Sighing; mad at myself for holding on to this stupid, ridiculous hope, I climb back up the tree. I scribble one last note.

I'm sorry you didn't come. I don't know why you didn't, but I just wanted to tell you that I understand and I'm not mad and …

The idea comes to me just as I'm writing it.

And I wanted to say thank you for giving me the watch thing. It seems like it must be a lot more valuable than the notebook I gave you. So, I'm going to give you another present. Something brand new and worth something. Maybe worth as much as the watch. But I understand that maybe you won't want to come back to the tree to get it. Maybe you'll be worried that I'll be up here waiting for you and it will be awkward. So, here's my idea. I'm going to leave something for you, hidden, in a place that isn't here.

I stop to think. It would have to be somewhere in West Hobart where I could leave it, in public, where Nyx could run in and grab it, and then run away …

I have an idea.

I'll leave it at the lookout at Knocklofty Reserve. Just at the bit where you look through the trees and you can see the Wrest Point tower. I'll leave some sort of marker there – I'll make sure you'll recognize it.

And you don't need to reply to this note or give me a present in return or anything.

We can pretend this whole thing never happened.

But I wanted to leave you the present. So you'll

know there are no hard feelings. And so you might
remember me and this thing we had that's a bit like
being friends.

I put the note into the Mailbox Tree and climb down again. And I reach behind my neck and unclasp my silver locket – the locket Mom and Dad gave me for my birthday, not long ago. It's still very new and shiny, like it's just come out of a gift box. It has a picture of me and Mom and Dad in it and I consider, for a moment, taking it out, in case that's too weird. But I decide to leave it in. I kind of want Nyx to at least know what I look like, if she doesn't already. Maybe she'll see me and realize I look okay. I look like … a friend. Maybe she'll realize I'm not a complete weirdo, after all.

I put the necklace in a folded-up piece of notebook paper, and I begin the hike up to Knocklofty. I know Mom will worry when I am late home, but I have to do this.

Nyx

It's 6.05pm and Bea's not here. I'm trying not to cry, but it's hard. I've been looking forward to seeing her all day. Real friends are hard to keep because no one ever sees each other anymore, and it's too hot to meet up. *All the friends you need are online.* That's what the chat rooms all say. Time has crawled by and I've wondered what she looks like the whole time. Dark-haired, dark-eyed, brown and freckled and dusty like me? *A bitser*, as Dad calls me, when he isn't in a mood. Or one of those fancy kids whose parents never let them go out under the sun? Paler than paper and almost see-through?

But it's just me here, under the Mailbox Tree.

No one's up there, on my branch. I know because I looked up through the branches as soon as I got here at 5.45pm, desperate not to be late.

I'd thought we could climb up and sit there together and just talk.

I climb up now, the resin oozing out of the branches, making my grazed hands all sticky.

It's so hot today, I feel physically ill. There's a thrumming in my ears and in my blood like a warning that I shouldn't be out. Like there's something squeezing me tight, around the middle. It's so hot that the air seems to be burning my lungs from the inside when I breathe in. My heart is so loud in my ears it sounds like a machine. When the weather is like this, over fifty degrees when the sun and the gusty, gritty winds are up, people try not to go outside, for anything, even for money or a dare. But I came out – just for Bea. And I feel so disappointed, I actually blink back tears. I've got no tears to spare. I've had nothing to drink all day.

Even now, when it's supposed to be nightfall, the heat of the whole earth is radiating right up through my bones, frying me as I climb. I shouldn't be here. If Dad knew, if he still cared where I was, he'd scream at me to *get away home!*

I look at the crummy old biosynth watch I found discarded in Dad's bedside table. It's so floppy and loose that it fits like a bangle. It could fall off any moment. It now says 6.13pm.

She's not coming. Face it, Nyx.

When I reach my branch, *our* branch, there's no one there. And I haven't brought any of that 'Neverending Story' paper because I expected her to be here.

I've got nothing to write *Why?* on.

And

Why didn't you come?

Why don't you want to be friends?

Why is life so <u>unfair</u>?

Just *Why?*

But then it occurs to me that maybe she didn't see my note from yesterday because something – like the Tasman Bridge going down, a pretty big *something* – could have kept her from coming here today. Like how my dad has been in a fit of towering rages all day and it's best to keep away when he's like that. Yelling at the shipping company, then the Citizens Police. Then at something called an *insurer*, and an *ombudsman*. Just yelling all day and forgetting to eat, so that I was forced to get him and me something just-add-water-to out of packets and him not even seeing me as he shoved rehydro into his mouth and turned his back on me to shout some more. I'd really counted on Bea being here. It had kept me going all day. Through the rages.

Dad never used to be like that when Mom was here but as Dad tells me, almost every day, *everything's changed.*

"Just not how much I love you though," he often adds.

I get that Dad's rages come less from anger and more from him being sad, worried and lonely, even though there are two of us still in the house. But getting that doesn't make it any easier.

A fat tear, then another, falls out of my eyes and through the branches of the Mailbox Tree, disappearing out of sight. I imagine the tears sizzling on the hot ground, nothing left but salt in one second flat.

I shove my hand into the knot in the trunk and sit up straighter as I finger what is in there, the smooth edges of fat folded pieces of paper. Bea was here after all! Maybe she just came too early.

My fingers shaking slightly, I pull out the wad of paper and I see it isn't the torn note paper from the 'Neverending Story' book that I left Bea yesterday, it's sheets of paper scrawled all over with Bea's writing, as if she wrote the words in a big hurry.

My eyes widen as I read the words *Knocklofty Reserve*.

Nobody *ever* goes there. It's dangerous, just this burnt out, toxic hilly area filled with twisted, dead trees and fallen down picnic tables, thin trails like scars running all over the reserve, acres and acres of dead land, like how the whole world might look one day if the bushfires get everything or the floods Dad's always raving about don't cover everything first. I know where the lookout is, but there's nothing to see from there. I've never heard of a 'Wrest Point Tower'. For a second, I feel uneasy. I wonder if Bea's even from here. There's no such place. I've lived here my whole life; I would know about something as grand as a tower. Nobody around here has any use for a tower.

But I shove the note into a pocket of my pants and climb down, also shoving down that uneasy feeling. She wants to be friends! That's the feeling I hold onto. She just got the time wrong and she's gone up ahead to leave me something, and maybe I'll catch her on the way there if I run fast enough.

It's actually too hot to run, everything is sticking to me – my hair, my clothes, the air in my lungs, even Dad's crappy biosynth band – but I do. I run through West Hobart as I catch the flick of shutters and curtains as people watch me go tearing past, trying to outrun the hot, stinging, gritty wind.

I run and run, the air burning as it goes in and comes out. I could be the last person on Earth as I burst out of Salvator Road into the wasteland that some joker has called a 'reserve'. What's it even for? Why reserve a huge, rambling parcel of dead and useless land? For what?

When I get to the lookout, that feeling I felt at the Mailbox Tree comes back, twice as hard, like a punch to the guts. Of disappointment and sadness.

She isn't here. I'd looked for the back of a girl – maybe a girl like me, my height, my age – disappearing up the scarred tracks ahead, all the time I was running. Wondering if she had dark, curly hair like mine, or the opposite. It wouldn't matter, one way or another. But Bea's a ghost. If she's here, she's invisible, because there's nowhere to hide. There are just a few broken metal stumps where the lookout fence used to be. It's been busted for years, and no one brings their kids up here because if you fall from here, you're dead, with no one to find your body because this place looks like it's been nuked. Like I said – a dead place. Finished.

I spin around and can't see any marker that Bea might have left, anywhere. The whole of the lookout is cracked and torn up. Concrete, steel, wood, all of it's no longer whole. I only know it's the lookout because it's high up, and Dad told me never to come here because the lookout hangs over a cracked and broken area that maybe used to be a parking place for people's Autos. There's a ghost town of broken-down tables and chairs and things he called *bubblers*, right next to it. When he described them to me, I couldn't even imagine free, clean water, available for anyone at the touch of a button. He told me this place was haunted. And looking down at it now, I believe him.

I get down on my hands and knees, sweeping across the damaged, soil-covered platform with the palms of my hands. There's nothing here. No freshly disturbed ground or things hidden around the sticking up boards.

If Bea said she was going to leave me something, made me run up here, all this way, to this horrible place, and then didn't … then she's *cruel*. She's not a friend at all.

I wonder then, if she did see me at the tree, and maybe didn't like the way I looked and decided to play a trick.

I sit back on my haunches, every part of me burning,

smearing dirt across my face as I push my damp, heavy hair out of my eyes. I can't help the tears that leak out of my eyes as I survey the broken teeth of the lookout fence. Dad is going to *kill* me for getting back in the dark. It'll be dark really soon and I've *ages* to run home. But the heart's gone out of me and I don't think I can run back to the sound of Dad arguing with people I can't see. I'm too tired. I feel hopeless.

That's when I see it. At the base of the central lookout post. A long skinny arrow, pointing down, scratched deep into the steel.

As I crawl closer, I can feel myself frowning. The arrow looks weathered and ancient, the scratches filled with soil and red rust. If I hadn't been down here, on the ground, blubbing, I never would have seen it. There are so many scratches in the old busted post, the arrow was almost camouflaged by hearts and letters and graffiti tags. But the scores are so deep and even that I spotted it. It looks like it was scratched in a century ago! But looking around, it's the only marker I can see anywhere, so I start digging through the loose soil at the base of the post with my bare hands until I hit something that feels like wood.

By now, my nails are all broken and I've got painful scratches on all my fingertips, including up under my fingernails, which I hate. They are going to sting for days. But I keep feeling around because I know Bea didn't lie. She *was* here. I know it.

There's a tiny gap between the base of the post and the wood that someone laid around it. Maybe a finger wide, that's all, where whoever laid down the wood didn't measure something properly and just one side hadn't sat flush up against the base. The side right under the arrow.

Still afraid that I'll feel snakes or spiders, or something worse, I keep scratching around inside the gap. In the space between the post and the wood, I can feel packed soil under my fingertips, pebbles, then something hard, maybe the size of my thumbnail.

I draw it out slowly, and realize I'm not breathing.

It's a rusty little heart on a chain. So dark and stained that I can't tell what metal it's made of.

I turn it over and over in my hands, feeling the small, domed shape of it. It's a necklace; I know that because Mom had worn one, something her great grandma had once given her. Grossly, it had had a lock of real human hair in it. It had come from the great-grandma's own grandma and had been older than anything I've ever seen or known of since. When Mom died, it just disappeared. Dad had muttered something about it being a *valuable museum piece which should be preserved for generations to come*. I'd just wanted it because Mom had used to wear it next to her heart and I could have worn it next to mine, too. But Dad had taken it, like he's about to take the rest of my time in this place. Without even asking. I don't understand how adults can do that. Treat us like things that can be moved around: *Sit over there! Go stand in the corner! No one asked you for your opinion, did they? This is all for your own good.*

Maybe this thing in my hands is like that? A valuable museum piece? I feel around the edges of it and it's so rusty, I can't tell. I'll need to take it home and clean it, to know; maybe find a blade to get it open. It looks like it might have something inside. I hope it isn't hair! I don't think I could cope with that, even if it's Bea's.

I close my hand around the rusty heart and turn to run back as the last of the sun's light vanishes. I don't know why Bea left me this old thing, but it must be important? I feel sort of happy, but grossed out, at the same time.

As I get back onto the path, there is a noise behind me, among all the dead trees. A sort of quiet scuffling, and then the noise of a twig snapping and something snaps inside me when it does – not like a bone snapping, but something in my brain and what's left when I hear that *snap* is just shuddering fear, like my nerves have been rewired in the wrong order. I look around me, anxiously, but I can't see anyone there, especially someone like Bea.

It doesn't mean that's true, though. It doesn't mean there isn't someone hiding among all the dead branches. And the thought makes me run away harder, faster. So fast I can't feel the heat rising up through the ground, through me.

Bea

There is no note when I go back to the tree.

My heart feels small. Shrivelled. Date-like.

I wanted so badly for there to be a note, this time.
I wanted to know what she thought of the necklace.

I wanted to know if she still likes me and wants to be
friends, even after all the things I said, all my feelings out
there for the world to see.

But I guess …

Either she got it and didn't like it or, for some reason,
she didn't get it at all, and I guess …

There's only one way to find out.

Back in the forest, the light is dwindling, becoming
silvery – the color of frost; of the fur on a midnight
possum.

There are more shadows; more dark spaces between

the green of the trees. Far off in the distance, Wrest Point is lighting up – so many windows like so many stars and the universe is now cylindrical.

It's very cold.

I wish I'd gone back to the house; pulled on my puffer, or at least another hoodie before coming up here.

I wish I'd waited until morning.

So many shadows.

But I had to know.

I reach the spot where I left the necklace and see the freshly scratched arrow that I made yesterday using a loose stone for a tool, making the cuts as deep as I could, freaking out the whole time that someone would see and say, "Hey, kid! What are you doing?" My heart begins to beat more quickly as I notice that the small mound I made beneath the arrow is still there, exactly how I left it.

My face flushes in misery. She hasn't been.

I dig with my fingers, making them gritty and dark. The dirt slinks beneath my nails and makes my fingertips feel tight and wrong. I dig and dig until I hit the necklace I buried yesterday, to keep it safe, for Nyx.

I lift it up and look at it, it's still shiny, but covered now in crumbly soil.

And part of me wants to take it back but another part says something's happened at her place that has stopped her from coming.

And I put the locket straight back into the ground.

She's going to come and get it, I have to believe that. And I realize in that moment how much our strange friendship has started to mean to me. Because I have nobody else. Because the thoughts inside my head are so loud and big and my skull feels so tightly wrapped around them and when I wrote to Nyx it was like I had a release valve. Like I had room inside my head for something else.

Something like … maybe even *happiness*. But she hasn't got the necklace yet and –

There is a sound behind me.

A scuffling, in the bushes, and then a snapping twig and my nerves are on fire.

And there are so many shadows under the green leaves.

I make myself small.

I don't know why. I should run. I should run, fast, all the way down the hill and home, but I make myself as small as I can and I wait, barely breathing.

Something is there.

I wait for it to come for me but there's nothing here but the night sky overhead, all the stars, and the sound of my ragged breathing.

"*Nyx?*" My voice is tentative, terrified, but all I hear is the sound of footsteps running away down the slope and I spring to my feet and follow that sound until, abruptly, it stops. But I keep running. All the way home, heart pounding.

Nyx

As I'd run home, I'd imagined I'd heard footsteps echoing mine until they'd ceased, abruptly, halfway down the slope, all the weird twisted trunks of the dead trees looking like starved and half-buried people, their withered arms raised toward the sky.

I'd broken back out onto Salvator Road in a lather of sweat, seriously spooked, my breath sobbing in my throat. The night seemed haunted, every hair on my body standing on end. If Bea had been there, she'd been hiding from me for some reason. Maybe there's something wrong with her? More probably with me. Maybe she'd seen me and been disappointed at my uneven hair, which I cut the ends off by myself because *cutting hair is not a job for dads*, my worn-out clothes – that haven't been replaced since before Mom died – and my dirt-streaked face, arms and legs. I'm just … brown. The brownest kid in my class. People tell me that all the time, which is right before I put them on *mute* and do something else. The world's brown, get over it.

The rusty edges of the heart necklace Bea had left me had cut into my hand as I let myself into the kitchen. Dad was still roaring into the space in his head where calls to official channels are made, still arguing for a *definite departure time* and *full compensation*. He never heard me walk in and grab a bag of rehydro, shaking it into a travel mug of barely boiled, rusty water and letting myself out again; the 'Neverending Story' notepad and a ten-year-old pen from the time when Mom still wrote me notes and left them everywhere, clutched in my other hand.

I scull my hasty, liquid dinner on my way back to the Mailbox Tree, leaving the mug beneath the Schustermans' back fence as I crossed into the old sports oval. I'll have to remember to get it on my way back.

The night is still hot, but I find myself shivering uncontrollably as I throw myself up through the familiar branches of the ancient old tree, heading straight for that knot.

Why hadn't Bea shown herself, up there at the lookout? I could have used her company. Someone friendly. Being up there was the bravest, and scaredest, I've possibly ever been. I put my hand into the knot and nothing is there. Disappointment is all knotted up with nerves in my belly. Maybe she's being mysterious on purpose? But why?

I open the 'Neverending Story' notebook, the rusty old necklace draped across one leg, and hastily scrawl:

I found your necklace.

It was really rusty and dirty. Does that mean something? Is it old and valuable?

I haven't been able to get it open yet because it's all clumped together with soil. Was there a reason you left me something so old? When I picked it up, I thought I heard footsteps that might have been yours. But I didn't see you, and I was really scared, so I ran straight home. It was so dark. And all the dead trees look a bit like screaming people. The whole place smells and looks burnt, like nothing will ever grow again. I've never gone there by myself and I don't know if I can go back. Not even for you, sorry.

I came straight here, to the Mailbox Tree, after I got home, because I was starving and I needed to get this paper and this pen, thinking you'd be here waiting. But you're not here either.

Can you let me know if you're even still in West Hobart? Or have you left for the Northland already?

Dad's still waiting for the first cargo out of here. So we still have a few days to meet up, if you want to? But no pressure.

I'm happy to meet anywhere you like, except not at Knocklofty. Everyone says it's haunted. Everyone in West Hobart avoids Knocklofty like a plague because it's all already dead. After the bad fire that took it out – someone illegally dumped barrels of chemicals and they caught on fire – it did something to the soil and stopped things growing, possibly forever.

Maybe we can meet somewhere more central? If you don't want to meet here.

Just let me know where and I'll be there? Dad's so busy trying to get us out of here, I feel like he sometimes doesn't even see me.

One day, when I'm old and can do what I want without asking, I'll come back here to live. Even if it's 100% desert, or 100% flooded, and all that's left to stand on is the haunted old summit of Knocklofty Reserve or kunanyi (aka Mount Wellington), I'm still going to come back. It will always be home. Even if home has to be a boat, or even our tree! Because I know our tree will still be here.

Write me? I'm a ~~little bit~~ lot confused.

Nyx

I study the tangled and dirty old necklace under the harsh moonlight filtering through the branches of the Mailbox Tree and shake my head in bewilderment. I still want to be friends with Bea, so, so much. But I don't understand what any of this means. I wouldn't give anyone a present this crusty in, like, a million years. I'm trying not to feel hurt by it. Couldn't she have at least, like, cleaned it?

I try to prise the heart-shape open with my fingers but nothing happens except for some caked old soil falling off it, and me breaking another nail.

"*Nyx!*" I hear Dad shouting faintly in the distance.

"You're scaring me, honey! Come home now!" Oh no, he's worked out I'm not home.

"Coming, Dad!" I shriek, my voice carrying across the dead old sports oval as I race home with the necklace, the notepad and the pen, completely forgetting the travel mug by the Schustermans' fence until Dad is locking the back screen door behind me, his face all twisted up with worry.

Bea

It's possible she's lying. I think this as I read her next note. I was there, yesterday, and she hadn't picked up the necklace. I was holding it in my hand. I'd buried it, unburied it, then buried it again, my heart like this heavy stone in my chest.

But in the note, she's got it, and the locket is … messed up. She can't even open it.

Is she playing with me? Pulling a prank? It's possible the note writer isn't even Nyx, at all.

She could be one of the kids from school, messing with me.

It would not be the first time.

But …

But there is this *thing* around my wrist, which I don't even have a name for, that might have been made especially for Nyx.

And there is the level of detail in everything she's said. I think of the way she described Knocklofty Reserve – like something after a nuclear war, all burnt and twisted and dead – and shudder.

Nobody at my school is smart enough to make something up like this.

And I was raised on *Doctor Who*. I don't believe in the TARDIS or Time Lords or anything like that, but when you grow up watching time travel happening in front of you every week, maybe the idea of it does crawl into your brain, a bit. Just the faintest inkling of a *what if*.

What if it's possible?

Nyx keeps talking about all this stuff I don't understand. Stuff that makes no sense if she's *now*. And the maddest thing of all of it is … I feel like I can feel her.

Or *someone*.

Near me. Close. Breathing. I catch the scent of someone, or I feel a tiny breeze around my cheeks, as if someone has run past me.

And then there were the footsteps, up at Knocklofty …

There was nobody there.

But I could hear them. I could *smell* them. I'm doing

my own head in thinking about it all. It feels like my brain is going to explode out of my nose.

Dad notices, because of course he does.

He's in the middle of packing up the kitchen when I walk down. All the various, oddly-specific kitchen implements he's picked up over the years, during his 'cauliflower rice' phase or his 'smoothies' phase or his 'smashed potato' phase.

A chill runs up my spine as I see him put his slow cooker in a box. If Dad's packing the slow cooker, we really must be moving soon.

"Hey, you," he says, looking up as I open the fridge. "You won't find much in there. We're going out for tea tonight, remember? Tea and the theater." He rolls his eyes. "La di da." His smile drops a little bit as I turn to face him. "What is it, kiddo? You usually love the theater. And I've heard good things about this production. You liked the movie …"

"Dad, it's fine. I'm keen to see the show," I tell him. "It's … don't worry. It's just other stuff."

"The move?"

I shrug and don't answer. Because, I guess, it is about the move a bit, in the way that it's *always* a bit about the move. But it's more than that, now. It's *new-friend-who-may-be-from-sometime-else* more than that.

My dad watches *Doctor Who*, too, and has done since he was a kid – way back when it was the dodgy Sixth Doctor. He's as much of a nerd as I am about this stuff, but he's also a grown-up and in my experience, grown-ups are less ready to believe in the potential of extraordinary occurrences.

Also, he's my dad, and he's totally overprotective and if he gets the slightest *whiff* of me being involved in something potentially weird or *dangerous* (because, you know, time travel does often seem to go hand-in-hand with danger), he'll have me on lockdown in a millisecond.

So, I paste on my best impression of a carefree smile, take two tubs of yoghurt from the fridge door and say, "Everything's fine, Dad. I just can't decide – vanilla or coconut cocoa?"

We eat tea at the Hope and Anchor, which is a really old pub, close to the theater. I have a chickpea burrito, and it's delicious, but I'm not feeling very hungry. I'm too preoccupied with thoughts of Nyx and who she really is; where she's really from.

When she's really from.

"You okay?" Mom asks me, when she notices I'm not eating.

Great. Now I have both parents on my case. "Fine," I reply, and take a big bite in the hope of convincing her.

She narrows her eyes and opens her mouth again. I steel myself for an interrogation but, thankfully, just at that moment, the alarm on Dad's phone starts up – with the *Star Wars* theme song – reminding us it's time to head to the theater.

When we arrive, Mom and Dad line up for tickets and I excuse myself to go to the toilet.

I don't really need to go. I just need a minute to myself.

I lock myself in the stall and sit on the closed toilet lid.

I stare into space for a few minutes, thinking about *everything*. And it's while I'm staring into space that I realize that the *space* has words on it. The walls do. And the door.

Years upon years of scrawled graffiti – a kind of amateur history of the common people of Hobart.

'*Craig Gordon – Hobart trip, 1969!*'

'*Steve and Nev, 1978 – carn the ~~Hawks~~ Pies!*'

'*I ♥ Savage Garden to the moon and back!*'

'*Tasmania banned guns – now let's ban Gunns!*'

'*Tasmania supports equal marriage!*'

'*Joey's Apple – friends forever!*'

It's while I'm reading the tiny snippets of Tasmanian lives, throughout the decades, that I have the idea.

I find a Sharpie in the pocket of my handbag. And I begin to write.

Nyx

I know time is running out. Dad said this morning that they'll have the first cargo up and running by the middle of next week and we'll be out of here. *Brand new life!* He'd said with relief in his eyes. *Brand new future! At last.*

And he'd hugged me. For a moment, it was my old Dad. From the time when Mom was alive and would pile straight into the same hug, if she caught the two of us doing that without her.

But I just want my current life, and preferably right here. But Dad's stopped listening to me when I start asking why we can't just stay. He hasn't noticed me not downlinking to school today because he's too busy running around the house triple checking we've left everything in order. I've just been in my room for hours, trying to prise Bea's rusty locket open with an old fruit knife that had belonged to Mom. It took me ages to chip away all the soil and rust. When I finally got the locket open, a few shreds of rotted paper fell out. I couldn't even tell what the paper used to look like. It's all a mystery – why Bea wanted me to have it, what the locket contained. It's the strangest 'gift', and I'm still bewildered that Bea thought to leave me something like this.

I wonder what she's like, the lady Dad talks to in his head all day when he's not shouting at someone official. I bet she's nothing like Mom. He loved Mom, but he was different around her. Quieter. Back then, he seemed to just work, downlink the news or eat dinner without talking much. But with this lady, Dad's louder and jokey and different – he tells her he'll take her out dancing and to dinner and to 'shows' when he gets to the Northland. Things that don't even exist here, in West Hobart. No one goes out dancing or to eat. Rehydros, and all the noise and fun you can have in your own head, stopped all that. No one *needs* to leave home anymore. I don't even know what 'shows' are. Mom told me she used to go to the Theater Royal in Central Hobart all the time, when she was little. She said it was already really, really old when she was a kid. And that it was haunted by a ghost called Fred, even back then. I'd shuddered at the thought.

But Mom's eyes had got really far away and dreamy when she talked about the 'plays', 'musicals', and 'ballets' she used to watch. I can't even work out what those would involve. I mean, I've seen bits of things like that in my head. But they're not very exciting, and I usually flick through to something else, starring someone #official. She'd tried to explain about people doing pretend things, wearing clothes that didn't belong to them right in front of other people who'd come together especially to sit next to each other and see them do that, and how alive that had made her feel. How watching a live show made her forget all about real life, just for a little while.

None of it had made the slightest bit of sense when she tried to explain it to me, to be honest, because most people don't want to be up close next to anyone these days.

I've never even seen the Theater Royal. Mom and Dad hardly went into Central Hobart, and they never took me there. "It's too dangerous," Mom told me once, when I asked if I could see the old building. "I don't even know if it's still standing anymore. It's a wonder someone hasn't set fire to it already, just for fun. We've set fire to just about everything else."

"Maybe the ghost is protecting it?" I'd told her.

Mom had looked very sad. "Maybe. But it's off limits, Nyx. I'm sorry. Wish you could have seen it, back in the day. The lights were so beautiful. It was like a jewelry box when it was lit up. Sparkling and bright. The things you could see there, on that stage. They were like actual magic."

As soon as the sun sets, I'm off. I tell Dad I'll grab my own rehydro when I get back and I won't be long.

He just raises his hand at me as he settles in to watch a movie with his new lady via a shared uplink. He's got his bowl of rehydro balanced on his small pot belly and he's already talking and laughing and staring into space as I let myself out. "Not long before we can do this together, love," he says, "in the same place!"

Ugh. I miss Mom, so fiercely, it's a sharp pain in my chest.

The night is still unbearably hot, like the inside of one of those mobile walker-dryers they used to shove us through at school, one-by-one, after we got out of the pool. I wonder if the pool is even still there, or if they've covered it over or filled it in, and whether the walker-dryers – a whole line of them – still work because no one ever goes swimming anymore. *Pools are breeding grounds for plagues!* the government told us a few years ago. *Stay safe by staying away!*

When people protested about keeping the last swim center in West Hobart open, the Citizens Police arrested some of them and no one swims anymore. At least not in public. And all of our highland lakes have been gone for years, and the lakes and rivers that are left are brown, or low or drying up, full of dead fish and discarded junk. Anyway, people are too scared of what's in the water to get in, these days. I don't miss the chemical burn of the pool water on my skin and inside my nose, but I do miss the feeling of being weightless and cool. It's not the same as the times I have a bath. The water comes out brown, just like the water in our rivers and lakes, and it's often already warm, even when you don't flick the hot on. I can't remember feeling cold anymore, and that seems … wrong?

I climb the Mailbox Tree, the rusty brown locket – as clean as I could get it – swinging around my neck and the 'Neverending Story' notepad jammed in one pocket with a pencil. I find I'm holding my breath as I draw out the folded note that Bea has left for me in the knot.

I frown as I read what she's written there and my skin gets instant goosebumps when I realize what she's asking:

There's too much to explain. Can you go to the Theater Royal, in Central Hobart, and look at the message I left you? I'm seeing a show there.

The women's toilets — on the back of the door of the first cubicle after you walk in.

I've left you a message. Can you tell me what that message is and what you think? It's really important. For you to tell me what you think. I have all these questions for you and I wish you could answer them in person, but I don't know if that's possible anymore.

I feel like I heard you up there, on Knocklofty. But you didn't see me and I didn't see you.

You have to believe that when I left you the locket yesterday it was brand new, it was <u>shiny</u>. My mom bought it for me last week. She put a picture of all of us in it. I just thought you'd like it and *would want to see what I look like. It was dirty because I had to bury it, but it wasn't old.*

Just read my message and come back here, to this tree, and write back as fast as you can.

I remember that feeling, up on Knocklofty, as if someone else was there, the sound of footsteps. There's nowhere to hide on Knocklofty, it's dead trees for miles around and every hair on my body, I swear, stands up as I re-read Bea's note. Why can't we meet up in person? What's the problem? The locket was the dirtiest thing I've ever seen and, even after a good clean, looks older than the locket Mom used to wear. And Bea's asked me to go to that exact theater Mom told me was too dangerous to visit now. But Bea's left me a message there and she wants to know what I think and I'm not a chicken, so I tear all the way home, lungs bursting, and roar as I pass Dad at a run, "Just going to bed, Dad! Real tired!" and he waves a cheerful hand at me as he continues chatting through his uplink with his new Lady Friend. He will have no idea about what I'm doing and I'm hoping it stays that way, just this once.

Once I get to my bedroom, I shove clothes under the blankets in the rough shape of me, then I tiptoe out through the front door – the front door we hardly ever use unless it's a doorknock by the Citizens Police or a nosy neighbor wanting to tell us what another neighbor is doing wrong.

I whisper, "Find Theater Royal, Hobart," and my voice-activated personal mapper comes on so that there's a faint overlay, behind my eyes of the fastest way to get there. You still have to be careful with the *persmap*, because it sometimes tells you to walk *through* buildings or *into* cavities in the ground that weren't there at the last downlink. Lots of people have been seriously injured, not watching where they're going while following a persmap, but my eyes are practically on stalks as I run through the streets of West Hobart. Then the persmap tells me I'm in Central Hobart now, and there are loads more Autos, and people on foot, some of them weaving around, all of them talking aloud to themselves and I'm suddenly afraid as I take in the rundown drinking holes, churches, shops, homes, all crowded together, storey on storey. Old buildings and new buildings and cardboard and found object shanties, all jumbled in a crowded, overhanging mess. There are so many more people in Central Hobart! I'm not used to seeing so many people at once. And all of them are screaming and laughing and raging at the voices in their heads so that it's like being in what I imagine a zoo would be like, but full of people instead. The world is just, what was that word I learned via downlinked school the other day, *cacophony*. The world is simply deafening. No wonder some people choose never to be in it, anymore.

"Watch it, kid!" a man in a stained shirt snarls as I turn the corner at a full run, almost colliding with him. I look up and see the front of the Theater Royal; a big, gray stone building that looks really, really old, with peeling wooden boards stuck across all its doors and windows.

I'm standing out the front of it, looking up and up and feeling hopeless and confused, while Autos and foot traffic cruise past me. I don't know how Bea got in there to leave me a message, but I don't think I'm ever going to be able to read it. There doesn't seem to be any way in at all.

"Kid," says someone beside me. "You wanna see inside? Take a tour maybe?"

I jump about three feet in the air. I can't tell what the person asking me the questions really looks like under all that hair, dirt and shapeless, tent-like clothing, which smells pretty bad. Shrinking back, I say in a small voice,

"I just need to see the toilets, that's all. Just for a minute."
I know it sounds crazy, just saying that out loud.

"Toilets?" the hairy stranger says bewildered. "Worst part about the place, they don't work. Why you wanna see the toilets for?" It could be an old … lady? By the shape of her. But I'm not one hundred per cent certain.

"Someone left me a message, I just need to see it." My reply is breathless.

If it's possible, a crafty gleam seems to come into the one visible eye that isn't covered over by a greasy fringe of hair. "What will you give me? To take you inside?" She points at Bea's rusty necklace around my neck. "That will do!"

Stricken, reluctantly, I give it up.

"Follow me!"

I take a deep breath and plunge into the dark laneway up one side, skirting the houses of cardboard, sheet metal and packing materials resting up against the side walls. People peer out at me as I stare up at the brickwork around me on which someone has scrawled the words *Sackville St* in drippy red paint.

The rusty stage door is sealed shut, but the hairy stranger, who is now wearing Bea's locket around her neck, produces an old key with a flourish and lets me through. "Go on then," she says, staying by the door outside and refusing to go any further. "Haunted," she mumbles in explanation. "Fred."

Fred! Goosebumps break out across my arms. *Leave me alone, Fred. Please.*

I try not to jump when the hairy stranger locks the door behind me again, from the outside.

With every hair on my body standing on end in fear, I murmur, "Toilets, Theater Royal," into my persmap, picking my way gingerly through scraps of rotted curtain and ropes and spilled-open sandbags, navigating my way carefully across the warped wooden floorboards of the stage by the faint light coming from my augmented vision. I come down off the stage and survey this vast, crumbling three-tiered space that soars up into a dome, a huge shattered light fixture lying in the pile of broken seats below. These must have been some of the magic lights my mom talked about. They look like they haven't worked for at least a hundred years.

Who would want to come to a place like this?

It's like a giant hand came down in here, sweeping through the rows of chairs, the giant curtains, the crystal and brass light fitting that's now in pieces on the torn carpets. I can't imagine how Bea could have come here to see a 'show', let alone leave me a message! The persmap urges me to walk up the side of the ground floor level until I'm out into a dark creepy space filled with fallen furniture. Maybe it had been a waiting room of some kind, or a place to eat. I can't really work it out.

"You have reached your destination," the persmap tells me quietly as I find the toilets marked with a stylised female figure on the door, in the shape of a triangle with a head.

"More light," I say as I tentatively enter the first cubicle and push the door almost shut behind me. I turn around and there are dozens of messages, many of them unreadable, erased by water and time. But my eyes are drawn to a message written inside a big black heart – the same shape as the locket I no longer have – which says in tall, thick, bold capitals:

BEA WAS HERE, NYX. IN 2023. WHEN ARE YOU?

My skin immediately goes icy.
Is that why Bea is never there when I'm there?

Could it even be … possible?

I look around desperately. There's a metal bar on the ground that maybe used to fit into the metal bracket on the wall of the toilet. I take the bar and scratch Bea a message in big shaky numbers. It can't be possible, what she's saying. I can't believe I came all this way, came into this scary place, possibly the scariest place I've ever, *ever* set foot in, just to see this. I'm confused and deeply afraid at the same time. But what if it's actually true? It would mean … actual magic has happened. Is happening. And our tree – our tree has something to do with it.

I don't remember what I said to the hairy stranger with the key to the crumbling theater as I knocked furiously on the inside of the stage door to be let out. After she'd locked the door behind me again, I pushed my way back into the cardboard and rubbish shanty town in Sackville Street before turning and sprinting all the way home, then past it, back to the Mailbox Tree.

Chest heaving, I write in shaky pencil on a stub of 'Neverending Story' paper:

I can't believe you made me go there! It was the most dangerous thing I've ever done on my own.

Ever.

Even worse than Knocklofty.

I wouldn't do that for many people, but I'd do it for you, Bea.

I left the answer to your question in the toilet at the theater which no one has seen 'shows' at for decades!

If you are playing some kind of cruel joke on me, I will never speak to you again.

But I don't believe you are. Please write back. Please.

Bea

It can't be right. *But it is.*

It has to be a joke. *You know it isn't.*

Someone is messing with me. *Nobody is messing with you.*

I'm going crazy. *You're not, though, are you, Bea?*

It's real.

This message. These words, which have to be written from a different time. It's why we keep missing each other, why nothing makes sense. The words are written from Nyx's *now*. This note is from a time in which the Theater Royal is in the scariest part of Hobart, and no one sees shows anymore!

I don't even know how to process that. How can I possibly process that?

And on top of everything – on top of the *wibbly-*

wobbly timey-wimey mindblowing madness of that …

She's confused.

And I can't let her be confused. Not only because of the *amazingness* of her being from somewhen else, but because … I like her. A lot. And you don't confuse your friends.

I hold the note to my face and inhale, deeply.

She *touched* this paper; wrote on this paper; but maybe she *hasn't done it yet.* Maybe she hasn't even been born to write this note.

It's the tree! Our tree is doing this.

I let out a swear word, long and low and satisfying.

Every single hair on my body is standing up. Every single nerve is on fire. *This is the most incredible thing that has ever happened to me. Ever.*

I have a sudden, reassuring thought. This note is proof that I am not what everyone at school thinks I am. I am not a loser. I am not a freak. This whole thing with Nyx might be unarguably freakish – unbelievable and strange – but it also makes me special.

There's an odd kind of comfort in that.

I shake my head. It's not important right now. What is important is Nyx.

She says she scratched the answer to my question into the back of the toilet door and I have to go see it for myself.

I shimmy down the tree and run all the way to the house; fling open the door. "Bea?" Mom puts down the plate she was drying and looks at me with worry in her eyes. "What's up?"

"I have to go back!" I blurt out. "The theater! I have to go back. I – I left my locket there!" The lies flow out of me with surprising ease. "In the toilets!"

I see Mom's eyes drift to my bare neck. She nods. "Okay," she says. "I know how much you love that locket. Give me a minute. I need to find my car keys."

Half an hour later, I'm back at the theater, in the toilets, staring at the door.

The door which looks exactly the same as yesterday. I know, because I memorised all of the messages and none of them are new.

I scan the walls and there's nothing to a *Bea* from a *Nyx*.

I feel a flush of pain so real, I put my hands up to my face.

My heart is a shrivelled raisin.

It's so quiet in here.

But as I stand there in the cold of the closed toilet stall, I realize. It's been one day in *my* time. Time is flowing through me to the her that hasn't even been born yet. It's why I can change things for Nyx, just little things, but maybe she can't change things for me. It's only the tree that lets us somehow … speak to each other. Across the flow, or despite it.

Mom is waiting in the car. There is a show on, and at first the ticket seller wasn't going to let me in, but I gave her a sob story about the missing necklace – again, lying with ease – and she let me in but told me to be quick. She said I had to be out before interval.

Which is in two minutes.

I need to go.

I'm about to open the stall door, when I hear footsteps inside the washroom.

There's someone in here.

And, of course, it could be anyone. Someone who couldn't wait till interval to go to the loo, or just wanting to get a head start, before the flood of theatergoers. But they're not coming into the toilet. They're just outside, wandering around. It could be the box-office girl. It

92

could be an actor. *Anyone.* But for some reason, I know it isn't. For some reason, the hairs are standing up on the back of my neck.

I hear a thumping sound – like they've dropped something.

They're just outside the stall I'm standing in.

That *shouldn't* freak me out. It could be anyone. Literally anyone.

But … something feels unnatural. There's a strange stillness in the air that feels *abnormal.*

I've heard the stories. Of course, I have – in fact, I think it was Dad who first told them to me. *Fred, the Theater Royal Ghost.* And ghosts are only in TV shows and books. But so is time travel.

A thought occurs to me. What if it's *her.*

Nyx.

The ghost of her, or the *echo* of her, reverberating backward through the years. I felt like she was there, at Knocklofty. What if she's here, now, too. But … it doesn't feel the same.

Footsteps, again. Moving away then coming closer again.

And another noise. *A metal sound, like a shaking can.*

Then the sound of pouring liquid hitting the ground.

I smell the petrol, its sharp acrid tang filling my nose as someone outside my stall laughs, harsh and staccato.

I know, more strongly than I've ever known anything – *I have to get out of here.*

I push out of the stall – before I can think it through – and then I'm running, running, running, toward the front door of the theater, and there's a voice yelling out behind me – "Hey!" It's a girl's voice. For a moment I think *Nyx!* but it's the box-office girl's voice. I turn and she looks so confused and I know it wasn't her who was laughing and splashing fuel and so – again, before I can think – I yell, "Run! Now!"

She must see the fear in my face because the angry furrows on her forehead smooth and her eyes widen and she nods and she runs after me, out the front door of the theater and into the bright morning. I don't stop. I run and I run. I hear her footsteps behind me, and then I hear something else. Louder than any noise I've heard before.

The terrifying boom and the clatter that follows makes everyone around me fall to the ground.

Then the sound of screaming.

I hide my head under my hands until finally, I take a chance.

I look up.

Smoke is pouring from the back of the theater and people are swarming out, coughing and yelling and clutching at each other.

The front of the theater looks just as it always has, but the back ...

The back is engulfed in flames.

Nyx

After I shove my scrappy note into the knot in the Mailbox Tree, I sit out on my favorite branch for a while looking at the navy-blue sky, lit from below by a customary tinge of pale orange. None of what Bea had written made any sense at all.

Bea's already sent me up to Knocklofty and left me a dirty locket with shreds of rotted paper inside. It had looked ancient and wizened, just like my heart had felt as I'd dug it out of the ground. Then she'd sent me to that terrifying old theater to find a cryptic message that couldn't possibly be true. But the thought hits me that maybe, just maybe, it *is* true and that when Bea had left that necklace for me, in her *when*, it really had been shiny and new and pretty. With a picture of her inside. I wish I could have worked out what she looks like.

I know that the theater I've just escaped from has to have some sort of relevance for her, but I can't work out what, because it's in one of the most dangerous places in Hobart. No one goes there unless they have to, and especially not to see 'shows' (you can see all the shows you want in your head, without having to leave your room or even your bed) or use toilets that haven't worked since the theater was boarded up years ago.

I turn the year she'd written on the back of the door over and over in my mind.

2023.

That was *seventy years ago*. No one in my life was even alive then. Not my Dad, not my teacher, not my principal.

I climb down slowly and head for home. She has to be playing a trick on me. But the little voice inside my head says, *But what if it's* not *a trick, what then?*

I don't sleep at all that night, because half of me says: *That's it, I'm not going back to the Mailbox Tree to be mucked around with, and lied to.* And the other half breathes: *This here is actual magic. Happening right in front of your eyes.*

The magic voice wins, because I do go back. The very next night, because Dad's uplinked with Lady Friend, putting the last of our things into movecrates, ready for the cargo to take by the end of the week, because we've finally got a leaving date. I need to know, before I go. If there's anything else. What it all means. To say goodbye.

The note that is in the knot in the Mailbox Tree causes my heart, it feels like, to stop. Just for the tiniest moment. The wind is so strong tonight that all the branches of the Mailbox Tree are shaking and groaning and I have to grip the paper hard to make sure the precious note doesn't fly away in the hot, whipping, whistling air.

There are tearstains on the crumpled piece of paper. It's made the pen run in places, which is how I can tell that Bea was upset when she wrote this. Her writing is messy and rushed, not the way it usually looks.

I know it's dangerous, when you are, but you need to go back, Nyx, and see the theater. Right now. Something bad happened today while I was there, looking for your message, which I couldn't find. I think I saw him, the man that did it. I ran right past him and had to go to the police station, to tell them what I saw. I was so scared.

I could have died.

When you see the theater, you'll understand that this is not a cruel joke. I know you've been thinking that. I have been, too.

I don't think you left me a message, or if you did, I didn't see it because – I can't believe I'm writing this – it's that you aren't even born yet, while I'm writing this. I think I can change things in your future because I'm back here, but I don't think it works the other way. Other than the notes you leave me.

I don't even know how that's possible but ... this tree.

Something about our tree is letting us do this. Talk to each other.

This is <u>real</u>.

Please let me know what you find.

And be careful. I can't even imagine what your world looks like, if Central Hobart is dangerous in your time. But at least I know this beautiful tree is still in it and that makes me so happy. That even after I'm gone, and you're gone, maybe the tree will still be here.

You and the tree are the only good things in my life right now.

I have to read the note at least three times to take it all in. If Bea is still alive, she's *old*. An old woman. Probably living on the Northland by now and someone who's forgotten all about me and this tree and this place. This … time.

I mean I understand this, that the things that happen in the past – my past – can change my future. But it really hits me in this moment, how true that is, because I can't change hers. Her future is already *done*. It's too late. But mine isn't. She can do things in her past that I might even see *now*, not where I am, but *when* I am. It takes my breath away, but for a moment, the half of me that doesn't believe any of this says, *but what if she's tricking you?*

Ignoring the voice, I turn the piece of paper over and take out the stub of pencil in my pocket and write:

Okay, I'm going back tonight. I am actually risking my life going out there after dark, but I'm going to run straight for the theater then run home and report back tomorrow.

A bit of me still thinks you're playing a huge joke. It's 2093, Bea. 2093.

I mean, I'm no good at science but I know none of this is possible. How can a tree be a kind of message bottle between two times? That's crazy.

While I'm out there, I need more proof.

You need to do something, as soon as you get this, that I will see when I wake up in the morning. I live at 7A Blackwood Avenue in West Hobart.

Do something in your when that I will see in my when, I dare you. It has to last at least 70 years for me to see it!

Nyx

Then I shove the note as far back into the knot in the tree as I can, hoping Bea will get it. Now that I know that maybe some kind of … magic is involved (*Is it though?* says that small, doubtful voice in my head), I feel less certain that she will get my note. Or if the magic will work. If the paper blows away, she'll never know I went back, just like she told me to, or where I live. And I'll never get my 'proof'. I wonder what she's going to do, if she's going to do anything at all.

I don't even need to bring up my persmap to find my

way back to the theater, which is still just listed online as *Permanently Closed.*

Like two nights ago, the streets are blazing hot and choked with dusty air, Autos and people, sounds and terrible smells; like choking cook fires and unwashed armpits and feet, rotting things.

I feel a crushing weight of disappointment when I reach the theater and look up at its boarded-up doors and windows. It looks exactly the same. Solid and sad and unloved, its best days long-disappeared. Not like a jewelry box at all.

When I duck into the alley that's marked Sackville Street in hand-painted letters, I see the same shanty homes, the same tired and dirty faces that barely look up as I search them for a familiar form.

The hairy person I gave Bea's locket to spots me before I spot them, sidling over. "You back again, kid?' Hairy Person says.

I nod. "Would you let me in again? For free this time because I've got nothing on me that's useful except a pencil?"

Hairy Person thinks about it for a moment then replies. "I need a pencil. Pencils are hard to come by around here. And that timekeeper on your wrist. Need one of them, too."

Dad's spare biosynth band. Hopefully he won't notice it's missing when I go home later without it.

I drop the biosynth timekeeper and the stubby pencil into Hairy Person's hand and she unlocks the theater door again, telling me, "Step carefully around the holes, mind."

I'm so busy telling my persmap to turn up the lighting and looking back at Hairy Person in surprise that I don't see that the part of the stage I'm about to step onto, just beyond the door, is *missing*.

"Whoa! Kid!" Hairy Person shouts, catching me by the back of the collar before I can fall through the empty air onto the concrete floor far below the stage. "I told you to be careful! Step on the *beams*. Geez, kid. Use your eyes."

I know my mouth is open because I can taste the ash and dust in the air.

"When I was here last," I say shakily, looking at all the burnt and missing parts of the stage floor, the huge black burn and blast marks up the walls, "the stage was *still here*." I'd only had to step around rotting bits of fallen backstage stuff like theater curtain and rope and sand on the floor. Now the wooden floor I'd walked across the last time is mostly *missing*. Only a few support beams are left to hold up all the thin air where the wood once was.

Hairy Person looks at me like I've lost my mind. "Whaddaya mean? It's been like this for decades. Arson attack in the early 2020s, been unusable since. Not worth restoring. You would have seen this the last time you were here, kid, just a few days ago. You're pulling my leg, c'mon."

Shaken, I ask her to let me out, back into the street, and she shrugs and says, "Your call, kid."

I run home all the way, still shocked at what I've seen. If I hadn't walked across the solid floorboards of the stage two days ago, I never would have believed it was the same space I almost fell through tonight.

Dad has no idea I've even been out of the house as I let myself back in, get changed and climb in under my blankets, unable to sleep.

I wonder what the morning will bring. Whether Bea has left me a sign, in the night, across decades.

Bea

When I think of a way to leave a mark, all I can see is a poem.

I know there are other ways, other *things* that a person might leave, to say, '*I was here.*'

The old kings and queens had statues, didn't they? Statues of their own *selves,* as if the soul of a person could be encased in bronze and made *eternal.*

Castles have stayed, sometimes. Sometimes, they stand proudly. Most often, they crumble.

I never want a thing I leave behind to crumble.

And besides, I'm no architect. I'm only a kid, living at the very underside of this burning world, in a time that, probably, no one will remember.

They won't remember me.

I won't be a queen. I won't build a castle.

But somehow, by some quirk or wrinkle in the universe, an echo of me *has lasted.*

It has lasted in Nyx.

She hears me, in 2093.

A whisper of my soul, in her ear, in *seventy years' time.*

That's better than a castle. I'm not crumbling stones. I'm *talking to the future.*

Because Mom trusts me, she's driven me here to 7A Blackwood Avenue, West Hobart, and let me out of the car outside a complete stranger's house. I see a small wooden house, which is already well over one hundred years old, with a sagging veranda that goes all the way around the front and sides of the house and a tin roof that's riddled with rust, sagging gutters.

In seventy years' time, Nyx is going to live here.

I look back at Mom, watching me through the front windscreen of the car, and give her a reassuring wave. She'd wanted to come down and help me explain to the homeowner what I was doing here, with this small tin thing in my hand. But I told her it was something I had to do myself. *Before we go,* I said, *I have to leave something for a friend.*

I'll only stay a moment more.

Taking a deep breath, I walk up the driveway toward the front door and ring the bell.

No one answers, even though it's almost dinner time and they should be home. Through the windows, the house is dark and there's no movement.

Stumped, I walk around the veranda and shrug at Mom. She waves at me to come back into the car.

There's no time.

Some poems take a decade to write. This one had taken only moments.

I'd written, on a scrap of paper:

I open my mouth and a vibration,

From my heart to yours,

Rises into the air and

Flies,

Across seventy years,

And you hear me, Nyx.

You hear my heart, my heart's vibration,

And even though the world is burning,

My voice remains,

Unburned,

My soul

Will not be turned to ash

And you

Hear me.

My echo, on and on,

And I wonder, if I echo forward, and you echo

Back,

How many other echoes are there?

Perhaps,

Somehow,

We can find the other echoes,

Make of ourselves a flock,

An army,

And somehow

Extinguish

All the fires.

I'd folded the paper, smaller, smaller, and squished it into the small metal tin I usually keep in my pocket for coins.

I wonder if Nyx has coins, if she knows what a coin is. Probably they pay with *thoughts,* in the future.

I scan the veranda for somewhere to leave this that will weather years and lives.

Under my feet, the wood is warped and brittle, but

they've been here for more than a hundred years and I can only hope they will still be here, in another hundred.

If any part of the house can survive, surely it's this part.

I crouch near the edge of the wooden veranda and feel around for a gap, a loose edge. And I find one. Where one piece of wood has rotted away and there's a rough-edged hole, almost wide enough to stick my fist through.

I take my tin and I slide it into the gap, listen for it to drop, hear nothing.

And then I run back to the car and Mom takes me home.

Back at the Mailbox Tree, I hastily scrawl a note.

Look for the gap in the floorboards, Nyx. On your veranda. About halfway up, in the front. There you'll find your proof. There you'll find a reason to believe.

Nyx

After I read Bea's note, I race home and onto the veranda. But it's already nighttime, past dinner.

It's too dark to know which hole in the floorboards she's talking about, but the first thing I do after I wake up the next morning is to open the small door around the side of the house and crawl under the veranda, crouching and puffing and crab-walking through the suffocating heat down there until I make it to the front. And then I see it, and my heartrate spikes.

A small rusty tin, smaller than my palm, rectangular in shape.

Emerging back into the sunshine, blinking, I try to prise it open with my fingernails but it's rusted shut, just like the locket she left me up on Knocklofty. The thing has sat in the mud and dust under the veranda for years and years. Washed by run-off, in the days when it still rained, and baked by the sun falling through the broken floorboards. For decades.

Inside my house, I get a knife and take everything into my bedroom and shut the door. Dad's actually out, for a change, even though it's dangerous to go too far beyond our neighborhood, because he had to go to the port where the cargos are to organise a berth with a bunk bed, for him and me, on the cargo that's going to take us to the Northland.

They needed biometric information, they said, for our security, and anyway, he had questions about what the uplink and downlink speeds were on the cargo. And about how soon we'd get off the cargo after we reached the Northland and how far the port would be from the house where his Lady Friend was waiting for us. Now that we're leaving, he's happy for me to do whatever I like, I don't even need to downlink any school anymore, because we're going. West Hobart, Tasmania, will soon be done. It's finished.

When I think about that, I get this hard lump in my throat that is impossible to breathe around, or through.

It takes me an hour to chip away at the rust until

I can get the flat tin box open. My heart is thumping madly as I pull out a curl of paper with ripped edges.

I tip it out into my palm in wonder. The paper is perfect, as if Bea put it in the horrible bashed up box that I've gouged into a strange shape with my knife just moments ago. The tin box took all of the bad effects of the time and weather. The paper isn't even yellowed by age.

When I read the poem, tears actually well up in my eyes.

I'm leaving all this – and her – behind.

Ripping out one of the precious last pieces of 'Neverending Story' paper I write:

Please leave something at my house that will live on, like our Mailbox Tree.

So that everyone that passes my house, even after I'm gone, will look up and wonder that something green and wonderful could grow in a hot, horrible dusty place like this.

Can you do that for me?

So that before I leave here, I'll see something that you put into the ground, for me, from a time before I was born?

It would really help me, us, I think. If you could leave something behind that shows that we were friends.

Leave random trees everywhere, all over my neighborhood, please?

Let's see who lets them grow, who lets them stay, long enough for me to see them. In my time.

Dad says one day there will be a flood to end all floods. That very soon, it's going to wash everything in West Hobart away for good. That's one of the reasons we're leaving. He says everything we take for granted, is completely doomed and we have to leave before we can't.

But even if a flood comes tomorrow that washes away every last person on Earth, I reckon our tree will survive. All our trees.

See if you can change my future, and yours. Even if it's just a little bit. Please help us breathe a bit easier? I know you can do it.

Nyx

I'm actually crying as I fold up the piece of paper and run with it all the way to the Mailbox Tree. If Bea can make my world, her world, even a little bit better, a little bit greener, it will mean something to me and all the people in my neighborhood who may wake up to find a miracle growing where nothing was growing before.

Bea

"Tell me again why we're doing this?"

Dad peers at me over the top of his glasses, a sparkle in his eye.

I can see he's excited – excited to be with me. Excited to be invited. And something in my heart breaks a little bit. I can see in his eyes lately, calculations – how many more times I'll invite him along with me, how many more years I'll want him around.

"We're doing this for *forever*," I whisper.

"What was that?"

I shake my head. "Wrong word," I say. "For the future, I meant. For the planet. For Tasmania. For the bees …" I wave my hand vaguely.

"Have you been watching Greta Thunberg on YouTube again?"

"Maybe." I press play on the CD player on the center console. It's one of Dad's favorites – a band called Fleet Foxes. They're singing about running through a forest in springtime and it feels right for what we're doing today.

I look around me, at all the green, and I think how lucky I am, we are. We live in the middle of a city and yet it's not gray here. It's not smog and grime and rubbish. It's so green. There are trees in every street and the mountain watching over us and ten minutes in every direction takes you to bushland.

There are so many trees here already, but mostly, in this part of town, they're European imports – gifts from the colonisers to make this place like home.

But this place is not England. It's its own beautiful creature. It deserves to look like the thing it is. And it's up to people like me to make changes for people like Nyx. She's counting on me. They're counting on us.

We have a car trunk full of tiny native trees in tubes, and I have a list of places to go that are all around Nyx's house. The house she will live in one day. I hope she sees at least a shadow of what we do today, me and Dad. It's taken days to put this together and it wasn't all me. It wasn't even half me. So many people – kids, adults, and my family in particular – have come together to pull this off.

I realize that it's the first time in my life when I've really had a *village*.

"I'm not sure this is strictly legal," Dad interrupts my thoughts.

"Any police officer who'd book us for planting a tree is asking to be on the front page of the *Mercury*," I point out.

"Fair call," says Dad, and turns up the CD, and the Fleet Foxes begin a song about mountains.

I look up at kunanyi and smile.

We cross the silvery water to the Eastern Shore, to Bellerive. By the beach, we plant our first tree.

At Risdon Cove we plant the next, and this feels somehow sacred. This place is a site of so much sadness, for the people this land belongs to. Planting something that belongs here feels like an act of repentance.

We cross back to the Western Shore again, and we plant by Gould's Lagoon. We drink tea and watch the waterbirds and I feel a surge of gratitude again.

I think of Nyx.

I think of her Tasmania. Is this lagoon still there? Are there still birds?

Despite myself, I start to cry.

"What's wrong?" Dad asks and I whisper, again, "The future."

Dad puts his arm around me. "It will be okay," he says, "because we're doing our part. And we will keep doing it, you and me, no matter where we are."

The last thing we do today, we go to Nyx's street and every second house, along both sides of the street, we plant a tree. Either right outside on the nature strip, if the owner's home, or inside the front yard, if they're not.

As the sun is going down, and we're driving home, I send a wish up toward the sky. That at least one of them will survive so that when she wakes up in the morning, she will see it, and smile.

Nyx

I'm woken by the sound of loud, frightened voices. Right outside my house. It sounds like there is a crowd gathered out there in the street, arguing.

Fear crowding my throat, I pull on a pair of shorts and my least stained T-shirt and run straight outside, not even remembering to call out for Dad, not remembering to shut the front door. Our cracked concrete driveway is searing and sharp with stones and bits of rubble under my bare feet.

The street in front of our place is full of people, talking, shouting, pointing.

"What is it?" I ask the backs of the people standing in my driveway, blocking my way so that I can't see what's going on outside in the road. "What's happening? Has there been an accident?" No one in our street can even afford an Auto, it's hard to believe something like that could happen here.

I tug on the T-shirt of a man leaning up against our broken gate but he ignores me. There are so many people standing out there that I can't move forward. I'm trapped.

My hand drops as I suddenly remember the note I'd left Bea last night. I look around my front yard and it looks completely unchanged. Disappointment threatens to strangle me; it almost feels like a wave crashing over me, or through me, cutting off all my air.

It's still a dusty bare patch of ground out here in front of my house.

She never came.

She never did what I asked.

It seemed such a simple request.

Maybe she didn't understand what I was asking?

Dad trails outside looking rumpled and sweaty and tired. "What the heck is going on, Nyxie?" he grumbles. "What's all this noise?"

His eyes widen as he takes in the press of people out the front of our house – more people than we've seen in one place since they closed that swim center despite the protesting crowd. Dad starts pushing his way through and forward. Because he's a big man, the people standing nearest to us make way for him and he's soon lost in the press of people. I collapse down on our top step, hemmed in by a wall of bodies and it's so hot now, the wind so dry and rushing it's like something that comes out of a machine, even though it's not even mid-morning yet. Even my butt, on the hot concrete, feels like it's sizzling in a pan. I squish into a small patch of shade near our front door and wait for Dad to come back.

I fall asleep where I'm sitting, because Dad has to shake me by the shoulder to wake me up. Cranking my eyelids open, I take in Dad's jittery, feverish expression. The way he looks is exactly when he can't get an uplink to his Lady Friend and things aren't going his way.

"It's a sign," he mutters. "A sign that we're doing the right thing by getting out of this place. Get up on my shoulders, quickly, Nyx. You need to see this. It's unbelievable."

I climb to my feet clumsily. Dad hasn't put me up on his shoulders for years. Not since Mom died, and I've grown a lot since then. "Are you sure…" I start to say but Dad crouches down and gestures wildly at me to climb on up.

Ducking to get under the lip of the veranda Dad pushes his way back into the crowd. People grumble as he pushes forward and to the right.

"Did someone have an accident?" I yell down at the top of Dad's head, the short brown curls shiny with sweat.

Dad looks up at me, his face bright red with the heat and the effort of keeping me steady up here. "Look out the front of the Magees' place," he shouts up at me. "It's unbelievable. People are calling it a *miracle*. Any way you look at it, it's a sign of unnatural times ahead. We can't move too quickly, Nyxie, we gotta go. Flood's coming. This place is cursed, felt it for years, even before your Mom and what happened to her. *It's a sign.*"

I look toward the Magees' house – this falling down timber place with ratty green netting in all the windows instead of glass – straight across the tops of all these strangers' heads and I actually scream in surprise as my eyes go up and up.

There's a *giant ghost gum* out the front of the Magee place, growing between the front fence and the road. I've only ever seen a picture of one. They used to be everywhere, one of my textbooks said, across the

Northland, here, too. I've never seen one actually growing and alive, *right in front of me.*

Its trunk is so wide that it's almost touching the falling down brick fence that Robert Magee and his family never bothered to fix when they moved in last year, or ever since. People have their hands on the peeling white trunk. Its roots are so big that they've broken up the sidewalk in places – a sidewalk that I know was treeless and unbroken only yesterday. Looking wildly up and down the street, I see that it's the only tree – a tree! – in the whole street.

A street that – since I've been alive – hasn't had a single tree in it. Nothing can grow here. There's no water to spare for gardens. Only rich people with money to burn have those.

I'm the only person that knows that Nyx must have come here – a long time ago for the crowd of people gathered around, *but only yesterday for me* – and planted this tree.

The tree wasn't here yesterday which means that today, now, all of us are seeing it for the first time.

"Witchcraft!" someone next to us mutters. "Black magic."

"There is no magic," someone else replies. "It's the end of the world, that's what it is. That there, is an act of God."

Dad looks up at me and turns around swiftly. "Flood's coming," he calls up at me. "This is proof – we have to be gone before it does. We're doing the right thing by leaving."

The crowd is so loud that no one hears me say, "The tree is a good thing. It's helping us *breathe*."

When we get home, Dad jumps straight into the rooms in his head, telling his Lady Friend about *The end of the world* and *The Flood*. I wonder if he's frightening her.

I grab my 'Neverending Story' notebook, terrified to see that there are only three pages left. Hardly enough space to tell Bea everything that has happened today.

I don't remember running out the back door, through the back fence, across the dusty oval toward our tree.

But when I'm in it, in our tree, when I feel safe again – even though it's only probably a fleeting kind of safety – I tell Bea everything that happened today in the tiniest handwriting. About how seeing the giant tree in our street, that hasn't had any trees in it for as long as I can remember, made me leap out of my skin, and frightened everyone who saw it. About how Dad thinks The Flood is coming and he's scared me so much that I think I can feel it, too. Even though the tree is good. It's right. Our world should be full of them.

The tree you planted was so amazing, my handwriting is so small and frantic I can barely read it, *that everyone took it as a bad sign that the world was ending!*

If that's really true, how do we save ourselves?

What will happen if The Flood comes while I'm asleep tonight and sweeps everything away and I don't even make it onto that cargo that's supposed to take us to the Northland?

If the Flood comes, who will save us? Where can we go?

I'm really scared, Bea.

My world is dying and I'm afraid it will take me with it.

It gets too dark to write soon. I only climb down from the Mailbox Tree when Dad comes out of the back door and calls my name, over and over, the fear changing the shape of his voice, so loudly that lights go on in all the houses around us.

Bea

I try to wipe away the tears before they smudge her writing, but I can't catch them all.

It still feels so *implausible*. Despite everything – despite all the warnings on the television and the movies about the apocalypse. Despite the scientists and the environmentalists and the Green politicians *yelling* at us to *do, something, now* ...

West Hobart is so beautiful – a leafy, happy little suburb on the edge of a wild and striking wilderness. In Nyx's time it is bent and burned and torn to pieces. No trees, no flowers. The lovely old houses battered and neglected and broken apart. A hollow, empty, ravaged place. Like a mind when a person has given up hope.

Like a mind when we realize that hope is being stolen from us.

The human mind has ways of protecting itself. If we all walked around, all day, terrified of all the things that might kill us, we'd kill *ourselves* out of sheer misery. The human race would not have survived this long, if we were scared all the time.

So maybe that's why we've been sticking our fingers in our ears for so long – humming to ourselves so we don't *hear*.

If we hear, the terror will overtake us so completely that we'll all just ...

Give up.

I don't want to give up. For myself. For Nyx. For any children I might have, or not. For all the animals who share our ecosystem, who have had no say in any of this.

I want to listen, now.

I want to help.

But it just feels like too *much*. How can one child save the whole *world*?

A voice whispers in my head, insistent:

"You don't have to save the whole world. You only have to save Nyx."

But how do I save her? The floodwaters are coming, she says, and she's stuck and the only way she could ever survive it is ...

"She has to go *up!*" I blurt out, suddenly, so loudly that Mom – in her home office – calls out, "Bea? Are you all right?"

And I know I should say, "Yes," so she'll go back to her work, so she won't be worried.

But the truth is – one child, *alone*, can't save the world and I can't do this alone, either.

And I really, really, just need my mom.

"I'm not okay," I call back.

She sticks her head out the door of her office, her brow furrowed. "Bea?" she says. "What is it?"

I meet her eye, suddenly realizing – suddenly seeing *so clearly* exactly what it is that we need to do.

"I need your help," I tell her.

"With what, honey? Your homework?"

I shake my head. "I need your help to build something. Up at the top of kunanyi. I need your help to build a safe house. For when the flood comes."

Nyx

Friday comes and goes without the cargo leaving, only because all of the north-east of Tasmania is on fire and all of the individual fires – either caused by random dry lightning strikes or by bored people with nothing else to do – are joining to become a massive fire front that's already swept down past Swansea, almost to Tunbridge. It's already taken out thousands of square miles of national forest, homes, shops, roads – even the 'new' Launceston airport which hasn't been new for at least fifty years. People are calling it *The Apocalypse*. As in the actual one – the one that's supposed to be at the end of the world. *This is it*, everyone is saying.

The cargo we were supposed to be on has been diverted to take survivors to safer places along the coast and carry supplies back and forth. Dad's so angry, I haven't heard him say anything in a voice quieter than a shout for the last two days. Most of our stuff is sitting on the wharf, baking in the sun, with the cargo nowhere in sight. It's good, but it's bad, too. I didn't have much stuff, but what I had, I really miss, because my bedroom is like a wooden box without a soul, or personality or any memories. It's just a space. I've only kept one of Mom's books, the rest of them have been packed away and are on the wharf. It feels a bit like I've packed her away as well. It doesn't feel *right*.

The sky is always red now, and filled with ash. It is a hell world.

Every day, I stand beneath Bea's massive eucalyptus tree for as long as I can bear it, sometimes with the rest of my street, feeling the oxygen slowly leaving the air. It's like we're all gathered together, waiting for our doom, like when Mount Vesuvius erupted in 79 AD and buried a whole town in ash. It feels like that with us, except that our doom seems to be creeping up on us and no one is trying to outrun it. There's nowhere to run to. We're going to be buried where we stand, beneath Bea's tree.

Dad's wrong about the flood.

We're not going to die from too much water

sweeping us away. Too much water would be a blessing. We're going to suffocate to death standing up in our bare feet, fully clothed. And every day I tell Bea exactly what's happening – that the fire is moving closer. That we need more trees.

That there can never be enough trees.

I ask her to plant more, every day. It doesn't matter what kind. Because maybe they will survive long enough to reach my time and make some air. For us to breathe.

We've been so wrong about everything for so long – pulling them all out to make way for houses and roads that look exactly the same and make the soil so soft and unstable that it just blows away. Mega shopping malls are the only things keeping us cool these days because no one can afford the power it takes to keep us cool in our own homes. And the grid keeps going down everywhere, for hours at a time on most days, because it's fed by a whole range of generators that don't talk to each other, or keep breaking down because of age or violent storms or because of raging bushfires like the one we're seeing now. Everything is broken. It's like we're camping in our homes, not living in them. Nothing feels permanent or certain.

The news about the building fire front is sometimes interrupted by the news of another miracle tree that has sprung up overnight in a suburb in Hobart, and some even further than that. But no one cares about Bea's miracle trees – I know they're all hers – because the fire is going to eat everything in its path and turn the whole of Tasmania into a twisted, burnt out, blackened space like the way Knocklofty Reserve is now.

Bea has told me how Hobart used to be green. And so full of trees and life that there were cool places, and shadows. There was even snow sometimes, in people's gardens. Now it's just scorched earth and nothing grows. Every day, I wish so hard for Bea's present to be mine that the wish almost hurts me.

There's nowhere left to hide, I write feverishly on my last piece of 'Neverending Story' paper in tiny handwriting.

We're too late, and there's nowhere left to run, anywhere on this whole island, Bea.

They say this fire that's bearing down on us from the north is worse even than the ancient terrible fires of 1967. That seems so long ago now that I can't even fathom what people looked like then,

what they ate, or how they dressed. What music
they listened to. All of that has gone up in flames.

The whole world seems made of red light and bitter,
ashy wind and 'There's no telling if we'll ever get
to the Northland!' Dad says, over and over, hugging
me tight. 'We're trapped. Trapped like rats here.'

I'm afraid all the time, I finish. *I don't want to die*
before I'm even old.

I'm about to fold the note and stuff it into the
Mailbox Tree for Bea when I remember to write at the
bottom:

PS I've run out of your proper paper. I'm going to
have to write between the lines of the last of my
Mom's old novels that I kept with me. She won't mind,
I think, but it will be harder to read, so I'm sorry.

The air is choking, as I climb down the tree and
I pull up the old bandana of Mom's that I've taken to
wearing, knotted around my face, so that I can at least
make it from our back door to the tree that is my lifeline
to Bea and a better, kinder, greener time.

I put my arm forward into the harsh wind, trying to
shield my face against all the painful particles suspended
in it.

Bea

"Of course I will help you," Mom says, pulling me close. She smells like butter and milky tea. "I would help you with anything. I will be here to help you for as long as I'm alive. It's my job. Your dad and me, both. That's what we're on this planet to do. Except …"

I sag a little, inside. "Except?" I ask, tentatively, wearily. I don't have *time* for 'excepts'. We need to build the shelter and we have to do it, now. "You're going to say, 'except this isn't realistic?' 'Except this is a crazy thing to do?' 'Except …'?"

Mom shakes her head. "I'll do it, Bea. Of course, I will. The only except is …" She scrunches up her face. "Okay, there are two excepts," she says.

"That's even worse," I say.

"Well, the first one, you have complete control over,"

she says. "And the second one, you have *half* the control."

"I do?" I say, dubiously. I'm a kid. I'm not used to grown-ups giving me *any* control.

Mom nods. "The first *except*," she says, "is that I need you to tell me why." She holds up a hand when I start to argue. "Beatrice, if you want me to do this for you – and, like I said, I would do *anything* for you, so if you really need this, of course I'll help – I need you tell me why. I need you to be *honest*, Bea. I trust you, always, but I still need to know why we're doing this."

I stare at Mom for a long time, right into her eyes. And I think about how I always have been able to trust her, how she's always had my back, how – even with this whole *moving* thing – she has always been honest with me. She's never betrayed me.

I can trust my mom, enough to tell her everything.

So, I close my eyes and I clear my throat and I tell her everything about Nyx and the future and *everything*. I tell her about the necklace and the real reason I'm not wearing it anymore. I show her the letters. I let her see the thing around my wrist that tells me the time and fits me so well it could be part of my body. I tell her all about the Mailbox Tree and, as I do, it's as if an enormous boulder has lifted from my shoulders. And, when I'm done, I open one eye, tentatively, and then the other.

And I wait.

And Mom looks very, very pale. But – I think, hopefully – not disbelieving. Not calling me crazy. Not rushing me off to hospital. Not calling Dad and telling him he has to come home *right now*, because Bea has lost her mind.

So, that's something.

But she's still not talking.

"Mom?" I ask, hesitantly.

She gives a little cough. "That's … a lot," she croaks.

"I know," I say. "A big lot."

"And you've been dealing with this, all by yourself?"

"Yep." There's a long pause and then I ask her, "Do you believe me?"

She breathes out, long and shaky. "I … would always believe you, Bea," she says, smiling as tears well in her eyes. "No matter what. No matter if you told me you'd been abducted by aliens or Bigfoot or … Harry Styles." This makes me laugh and it snaps the tension. "I believe you," she says, more quietly, as a tear drips off her chin. "It's madness but I believe you. And of course I will help you – like I said. Except …" She catches my expression. "I *said* there would be two excepts. Even more so, now. Hear me out, please." I nod. "*Except* … we can't do it alone. Not just you and me. We'll need council approval and a team of helpers …"

She holds up a hand when I make to interrupt.

"The council part, I can probably deal with. You know Auntie Deb is pretty high up on the HCC."

I nod, even though I had no idea that Auntie Deb was 'high up'. I thought she was just in charge of bins or escaped dogs or something. I nod, even though Auntie Deb isn't my real auntie at all – she's Mom's best friend from primary school. I nod, even though I don't have faith that any grown-up who isn't in my family could do *anything* to help with this. This feels too personal, too *part* of me. And Mom and Dad are part of me, but Auntie Deb …

I love her, but can we trust her?

Can we trust her not to spill our secret to the authorities – the police or the state government or whoever it is who has the power to veto this – and ruin everything?

As if reading my mind, Mom squeezes my hand

tightly and says, "I know I can rely on Deb. We sort of have a deal – we will *always* have each other's back. No matter what and forever. This is just the sort of thing best friends do for each other."

I think of Nyx and how I would do *anything* to save her and, suddenly, I believe Mom.

"Okay," I say. "Please ask her to help."

Mom nods. "And for your part, I need you to do something really brave."

My heart stills. I'm not good at being brave. I'm a complete coward. "What?" I whisper.

Mom clears her throat. "I need you," she says, "to get up in front of your school and ask your friends and classmates – and teachers – to help us build the shelter."

My heart stops.

Completely.

Irreversibly.

Because Mom doesn't know it, but this is the one thing I *absolutely* can't do.

Nyx

Sunday, and the world is still on fire, and all the people in it are fleeing south into our tiny part of Tasmania. They're saying it's going to get over the top of Cradle Mountain soon, that maybe only the sea can stop the fire now. The whole of Tasmania could be made of paper or tinder. It feels that way. It's frightening.

I'm clutching the new, plain blue notebook that Bea left me overnight, my bandana pulled right up under my watering eyes, the sky so dark and gritty I can barely make out the words she's written on the first page.

She's telling me she's got a plan, but it's going to be really, really hard because it means that she'll need to get help from everyone she knows, everyone at her school; even the kids who've been bullying her so badly that her life is miserable.

I can't even imagine how that feels, because since the fires started, school has been completely suspended, for our safety. It's funny to think of a whole school being suspended, rather than just one kid who's done something wrong or has been mean to someone else. But it's exactly how it feels – we've all been cut off from each other and now we're just hanging in place, like puppets that can't move.

I can't understand how anyone could be mean to Bea. I can't even imagine kids banding together, in one place, to make some other kid's life miserable. I don't even know the names of everyone in my class because some of them never show up for roll call or special classes we all have to uplink to, together, to hear someone speak. In my time, you can be as out there, or as hidden, as you want. Some kids are in the space behind your eyes shouting just like everyone else is, at everyone else. But others are like me, or worse – they put up a *Permanently Closed* sign, just like how that old theater is described online – and check out of chat rooms, check out of communicating, check right out of life. Those kids are like ghosts. I'm not one of them, but I get how hard it is some days to want to be seen.

I scrabble for the stub of pencil in the pocket of my shorts and write:

We're just hoping for a break in the endless heat. People are saying there's a real potential for rain next week. I can't remember the long, scientific name for the kind of cloud that a really bad bushfire can make in the sky, but one of those huge 'fire clouds' is building, TasGov is saying on the emergency news services, over the fire front. They're saying to stay away from the areas as much as possible and to seek shelter where you can inside. The fire cloud may bring rain for days, strong winds, ember showers. If the rains do come though, I'm going to stand outside in it while it pours, for as long as it pours. I can't remember the last time it really rained. It usually evaporates straight off your skin the moment it touches you.

There's also a big low-pressure system building over the Tasman, the Newsmedia says, because of all the heat from the fires. They could be wrong or just trying to scare us — it's hard to tell Fakenews and Realnews apart — but I'm really hoping that the rain will finally come and put the fires out. The more water the better, I say.

People are running out of food and space and hope, Bea. The Northland has just put hard limits on how many Tasmanians can be evacuated there each day. There aren't places enough to put us, not enough food to feed us. People are really sorry for us, on the Northland, but they don't care enough to want to look after us. They're already crowded enough and fighting for their own space and food and energy. Things are bad enough over there – they have their own wildfires on the go at the moment. Not as big as ours, but still bad – on the west coast, in the north. Dad says if this goes on for much longer, TasGov is going to put desperate people into our houses. To live with us. Anyone with a spare room is going to be assigned a family to look after. That's how desperate it is.

Let me know what the plan is? I'm out of plans, we're all out of plans.

Nyx

I climb down from the Mailbox Tree with difficulty,

staggering through the curtain of airborne dust and ash that's blowing across the bare 'reserve'.

When I reach home, Dad's not there. And there's something stuck to our back fence – a notice written on precious paper, like in the olden days – that says that the O'Donnell family is moving in, tomorrow.

Bea

Before we leave for school, I scribble a note, hastily, and post it in the knot in the Mailbox Tree.

I wipe a tear away – a tear of regret or anger or fear, I'm not sure which quite yet – and I join Mom in the car.

She glances over at me. "You sure?' she asks.

I nod, sighing.

Mom gives her head a little shake, and I don't know what that means until she says, "I'm proud of you. Always. This is possibly the bravest thing you've ever done."

And then, when I don't reply, she pushes some buttons on the steering wheel. A song by Josh Ritter. He's singing that he's not afraid of the dark, about beasts and shadows, and it's not the dark I'm afraid of, but I know why Mom put it on.

"Do you want me to come in with you?" she asks.

I shake my head. "You need to go and see Deb."

Mom nods. "I'll do my bit …"

"And I'll do mine," I say, attempting a smile.

She raises her hand for a high five. It turns into a hug, anyway.

I open the car door. I feel like I can smell smoke in the air. There are no fires around, so it makes me feel as if Nyx is sending me a message – a smoke signal through time.

She's saying:

"You can do it."

She's saying:

"Be brave."

She's saying:

"You have to do this. For me and for our world."

Mom already called ahead, to Principal Leitch, to explain everything (well, not quite *everything*).

Miss Leitch didn't quite understand and said she couldn't 'endorse' the 'initiative' until we had council approval.

But she'd let me speak.

"I feel like it's important," she said, "to let children speak."

And so, here I am, standing in front of the whole school. Leaning so hard on the podium it's cutting into my forearms. Leaning because if I try to stand by myself my legs will fail and I will fall.

In front of me is *everyone*. Every kid I've ever run from, every kid who's ever called me *freak*. Victoria is watching me, one thin eyebrow raised, waiting, *smirking*. Waiting. Everyone waiting. To hear what I have to say.

And what I have to say is madness.

Nyx

The O'Donnell family turn out to be two scared adults, who apologise for everything, and a thin, hairless baby who cries all the time.

Dad's trying to be as polite and helpful as possible, but because almost all of our stuff is sitting on the wharf, bundled off the cargo that is still ferrying people and things up and down the coastline away from the fire front, we should be the ones who are apologising. All we're offering the O'Donnells is a bare, hot and airless room with a tin roof over it. Dad and I are basically living off rehydro and in two sleeping bags. I don't think the Citizens Police knew what they were doing to the O'Donnells when they dropped them off here. I saw their faces fall when they came inside and felt so bad for them. It's been like this for days, and even I'm not used to it yet and I *know* why it's like this. Sometimes, at night, I put Mom's old paperback book under my head, even though it's uncomfortable because it's the only thing of hers that's still in the house with us.

Lucky the O'Donnells came with their own small movecrates of things, but every time Mrs O'Donnell tentatively asks a question like, "Have you got a serving spoon?" the answer is always, "Well, we did, but now we don't. Sorry." And I show her the empty drawer or cupboard where the thing used to be that now just holds dust and crumbs and her face falls.

When the O'Donnells go out looking for food to buy, they often come back with things that the baby won't, or can't, eat. And then she cries and cries.

It's been really hard.

The O'Donnells lived near Tunbridge, way further north, and they don't even know if their house is still standing. Those two small movecrates in our spare room may be all they have left in the world. Every night, I hear both of them taking turns to try and uplink to people they know or downlink any news that isn't about places outside Tasmania. But people from the north-east and the center have been scattered everywhere by the fires, and any news about Tasmania at all is just full of pictures of towering flames, burned people or burnt-out homes and Autos. I get that the Fakenewsmedia wants to show everyone else in the world that this is the end of the world at the actual end of the world, but it feels like it really is.

Mrs O'Donnell is in tears a lot, Mr O'Donnell, too. They try not to let us hear them crying, but our house is very old; with walls so thin and termite-eaten they could just be lacy curtains, not walls. We can hear everything. Sometimes all of the O'Donnells are crying at the same time.

Dad can't meet their eyes, and neither can I.

The day after they got here, I showed them the ghost gum that Bea planted and it made them both smile for a few minutes as they looked up and up into its branches. But then they remembered where they were, and why they were here, and they haven't gone out and looked at the tree since.

I'm sitting in the Mailbox Tree now trying to describe all this in a way that isn't boring for Bea. Nothing is ever good here. I wonder what she thinks of how I live. Whether anything feels the same, or if she feels sorry for me, the way I feel sorry for the O'Donnells.

I wish I had something good to tell you.

But even all the huge trees that keep appearing all over West Hobart (thank you!!) aren't considered 'Realnews' anymore. People who aren't in Hobart are calling them 'Fakenews' like the trees aren't actually solid but are Greenscreen trees. But I know different. I know that it's you doing it for me and the world I live in, and I'm so grateful.

I can't thank you enough. I just hope the fires don't come here and undo everything you've done, and keep doing.

I wish I could do something for you, but I don't think time works that way, from what you described about the theater. You're just paying it forward all the time and I'm just sitting here hoping that your acts of kindness make it into my present, so that I can see them. It feels very selfish. We have nothing left to give. We have nothing, it's true.

I have nothing good to give you anyway. The world isn't made of much 'good' anymore.

As I write that word again, *good*, I feel a drop of moisture on my forehead.

My heart rising, I turn my face so that I'm looking

up through the branches of the Mailbox Tree but it takes a while before I feel another drop.

Rain!

I start writing again, really quickly.

It's raining, Bea! Real rain!

It may only rain for a very short while — that's all it ever does, not enough to wet the ground even. But here's hoping that it will rain long enough, and in the right places, that people like the O'Donnells can go back to find that their homes are still standing!

It hasn't rained for months. Not since before I found your first note. We've been drinking desal water for years and using it in our rehydro, but it's so horrible the way it comes out of the tap (brown and salty) that we try not to use it unless we absolutely have to. I hope you have better water, in your present.

At least the rain will help to keep the temperature down and the tree you planted for me alive for a little while longer.

I'm going to climb down out of <u>our</u> tree now and stand in the rain.

At least it won't be the color of the stuff that
comes out of our pipes, for once.
Going to leave it here for now!
It's raining, it's raining, it's raining!
Nyx

I fold the note and leave it in the knot, climbing down so fast out of the Mailbox Tree that the new scrapes on my hands and knees immediately start stinging when I get out in the gentle, steady rain.

I whirl around a few times under the grayish, mostly orange skies with my arms open, until my T-shirt and my shorts are soaked. Even the notebook from Bea that I've slipped into the waistband of my shorts is starting to feel damp.

Slipping and sliding around in the mud with my bare feet I have to resist the urge to lie down in it like all those animals I've seen in pictures over the years – hippos and buffalos and pigs. I wonder if they all rolled around in this stuff together, how weird that would look. Were they all the same size? Maybe they never rolled around together because maybe hippos *ate* buffalos and pigs? All the facts I have ever learnt about long dead animals are a jumble in my head. They've been saying for years that science will bring them all back one day – Tassie tigers and Tassie devils, quokkas, koalas, hippos, buffalos and even non-genetically modified pigs, 'heritage' pigs (whatever the difference is), but they never have. The places all these animals would have lived can't support them anymore, scientists say, so we'd only be bringing them back to die out all over again and that would be beyond cruel. So we just haven't.

I stay out in the rain so long that it's full dark before I start picking my way back home across the reserve, trying to protect Bea's precious notebook from getting too wet, the rain falling heavier and heavier on my chilled body as I go. I haven't felt cold in a long time and it is the Most. Amazing. Feeling. I wish I could tell Mom. I wish so much that she was here.

Bea

Rain begins to fall on the roof of the assembly hall. First it comes slowly, hesitantly, a drop here and there like the beginning of tears.

And then the tears become a symphony.

Even though everyone knows what it is – everyone knows what rain sounds like and everyone knows we are sheltered and safe – most people look up at the roof. As if this time the roof won't hold. As if this time it's not rain but meteors or dragons.

I think of Nyx. I think of what rain must be like for her. Maybe, for her, it is as rare and frightening as dragons descending.

The only people who keep their eyes focused on me, at the podium, are the teachers and the bullies, and the bully girls who just stare, eyes made into mean little coin slots on their faces and a tiny dark piece of me wants to find some coins and *push them in*. But I don't, of course, and I don't let their cruelty get to me, either.

I think of what Nyx would do.

I think of her bravery.

I think of how the *world is ending, sooner than we think* and these girls? They don't matter. At the end of the world, we're all the same. Nobody better or cooler or more popular than any other person. Nobody will have more worth – not presidents, not kings and not those girls in front of me. And, after all, they're not the ones fighting to save the world, are they?

That's me.

That's me and Nyx and our mad, bewildering plans and I have to take the first step. I have to be the clouds, now, letting down the rain into a burning world.

Slowly, at first, then a symphony, a swarm of dragons. I lean toward the microphone and I begin.

"The world is ending," I say.

One of the mean girls rolls her eyes. Callie. "It's only rain, idiot," she says.

"For now," I answer, bravely. But one day, the rain will be worse. One day, soon, the fires will be worse, the tsunamis, the earthquakes. It's all getting worse. We have to stop it."

She folds her arms. "And how are we going to do that, weirdo?" The girl calls out. No one stops her.

"Yeah," says her friend. "If the world is ending, that's huge. Too huge for us to stop it." She scoffs. "Duh."

I let myself smile. Just a little bit. Not a happy smile but the smile of someone who has a plan, who might just make a tiny, raindrop difference.

"We start small," I say. "We start by building something for the people who will come after us that have to survive fires and floods, and worse."

Nyx

It's been raining steadily for three days solid, all down the east coast, not just here, and the cold and wet feel very much less amazing now. People are calling it 'miracle rain' because it's put out the worst of the fires in the north-east, although the fires in the north-west and the Derwent Valley aren't out yet and are moving steadily toward the west and south-west, tearing through anything that's still dry. All these national parks are under threat, parks with thousand-year-old trees and moss in them, and all we have to protect them with is aerochem. It would take days' more rain to stop everything that is burning. It would take Dad's flood to do that.

Dad often asks himself out loud whether it would be preferable to die by burning or die by drowning. And then he laughs. Cackles, actually. It's beginning to freak me out. The O'Donnells, too. He's started doing that a lot – talking out loud. And the voice he uses with his Lady Friend isn't the one he uses when he talks and cackles to himself. So I know the difference.

Even though the fire's out in Tunbridge, the O'Donnells haven't been able to leave here to return to their place yet because the ancient bridge near their home was burnt down, then washed out. Just the footings of the old bridge are left. The river there burst its banks so they are worried that there could just be a sea of ashy soil and debris where their house used to be.

Mrs O'Donnell spends her days wailing to whoever will listen that she is *cursed*.

But I think we're *all* cursed. Dad's walked out to get rehydro each day for the last three days for all of us and there's almost nothing on the shelves at our Megamart, or even further. He comes back with a handful of packets of the worst flavours that everyone in the closest six suburbs have already combed through and we inevitably have to share so that none of us in the house goes to bed with a full tummy. All the neighbors in the street have been swapping and pooling food – those who are still speaking to each other, that is. It's getting pretty desperate. The

Citizens Police may have to organise food drops soon because the shelves are mostly empty and most of our food gets sent across from the Northland now – we're just living on water and the weird rations they've decided will do for us; like bags of plain rice, lentils or flour that we've got no water or energy to turn into something else that tastes less like rice, lentils or flour. Anyway, as soon as the shipments get dropped to these places that most of us can't reach on foot, they're gone within a matter of minutes because desperate people get into punch-ons with each other to get to the bags. Almost a dozen people have died so far, just lining up for rations.

"Rations are for idiots," Dad told me and the O'Donnells gloomily once, as we worked out how to divide a rehydro-for-one of 'apricot chicken' (didn't taste of either, I'm pretty sure) and a rehydro of 'choco-pudding' (also not entirely convinced about its choco-ness) between the five of us, none of which the baby ate.

It was so wet yesterday that I couldn't get to the Mailbox Tree, and I wonder if Bea thought I'd forgotten to write when she went to look inside the knot. One of the giant branches of the ghost gum Bea planted outside the Magees' house fell down and took out the part of their front fence that was still standing. The Magees want to cut the tree down now because they are worried it's unsafe, and use it up for wood because everyone is fighting for wood now, too, it's so cold. But a whole group of us stood around the tree, in a circle with our arms linked, to protect it. It's been pretty tense in the street since then. Every morning when I wake up, I worry that it's gone – that someone's cut it down in the middle of the night and taken it away to burn.

I had to write my note to Bea indoors today because it's too wet and uncomfortable to sit in the Mailbox Tree and write anything now. I'm going to pray for a break in the rain and run out there with my persmap on, so that I can see my own feet. The night sky isn't orange-gray anymore, it's black and impenetrable and stinging. The rain has stopped being fun and helpful and refreshing now. It's just seriously annoying. We've sprung a leak in our bathroom. The constant sound of dripping is keeping me and the O'Donnells up at night. I hear them talking about how *life doesn't feel worth living right now*, over the sound of the drips.

I've spent all afternoon telling Bea where the fires are now, and where the water is, and how most of the population of Tasmania is fleeing from it and being squashed into this ever-smaller pocket in the south-east, where we are, or onto Bruny Island. The whole population that hasn't already shipped out to the Northland on private charter boats or FedGov shipping organised for evacuees, that is. I wonder if any of it is recognizable to someone in a present where there is more than enough to eat, and energy that comes on at the flick of a switch. I've never known a time like that, ever. Even when Mom was alive. Only Mom was reliable, and Mom's gone.

If the fires get here, too, we're doomed, I finish up now. *If we don't run out of food or drinkable water first.*

I finish by signing my name in pencil, like I always do, *Nyx*.

I jam my feet into a pair of Mom's old ankle boots that we'd found in a cupboard we'd forgotten to clear, because they're the only thing that fit me at the moment, all my shoes and flip-flops are too small or let in the water immediately. Then I jam the note in my pocket, take a deep breath in my old raincoat – also Mom's that is far too big through the sleeves and shoulders – and start wading through the ankle-deep mud toward the tree.

Bea

It started with one hand.

It took the longest time – years, surely. I stood alone, shaking, at the podium, my heart gone *beyond* my throat, my mouth – my heart having *leaped* out of my mouth. My heart now flying around in front of me, bewildered and ashamed.

Surely, everyone could see it. Surely, everyone could see my heart, just *out there* and soon they would start laughing, soon they would chortle and point and the mean girls would call out all sorts of things, all sorts of *names* for just the kind of freakish person I am.

Did it matter? It wouldn't matter to Nyx. Nyx would brush off the stares and the laughs and the names like a blowfly on her shoulder. It wouldn't matter, if the world ended.

But it *did* matter, because I needed help.

It was only a very small thing – this building of a shelter – but still, I couldn't do it alone. Even with my parents – they didn't have the money or the skills or the resources. My father threw Father's Day catalogues full of saws and wrenches in the bin with a sneer. He wasn't *handy*. Neither was she.

We needed these people to help us. I needed these people to want to help.

Because it *was* only a small thing, but one small thing leads to another. Incremental changes, as big as a shed on a mountain, make bigger changes, later on.

A butterfly's wings, in China.

The wings of a pardalote, in Tasmania.

This was just the start.

But it would be the start of nothing if nobody raised their hand.

And then – like a miracle – somebody did.

A boy in the year below me – black hair in locks, black skin reflecting the light.

His name was Adam, I remembered. The entire hall turned to look at him. He lifted a shoulder. "I'm good at building," he said, with no hint of meekness.

"I'm going to be an engineer. I can help with the design and construction."

The girl next to him – Polly – grinned at Adam and said, "I never knew you wanted to be an engineer." She turned back to Bea and raised her hand, too. "My dad has a lumber yard. I know I can get him to donate some stuff."

The principal, Ms Leitch, stood from her seat. "Bea, can we get a bit more information about why you're doing this?"

I scrunched up my face. I'd been dreading this question.

"I can't tell you everything," I said, looking at the floor. "Because some of it sounds ridiculous and implausible and ... it probably is *all* ridiculous and implausible but ... the important thing is that there's a girl called Nyx and she's my friend and she's ... in trouble. In the ... the not-now. The future. Which sounds completely like I've lost my mind but it's true. It's true and I ... I need you to trust me. I know I'm only a kid, but—"

Ms Leitch held up a hand. "Where's the rule," she said, slowly, "that says we should not trust children? In my opinion, children are the ones who should be trusted the most. And it's also my opinion that the strangest and most implausible things turn out to be the truest and the most important. I don't understand it but that doesn't mean I don't believe you." She turned away from me, toward the other kids.

"Bea has my full support," she said. She clapped her hands together. "Now, who else is in?"

The hands that were raised were like new trees, growing, forming an enormous forest. So many hands. So many helpers.

In the end, the only hands that did not help form the forest were the hands of the mean girls.

Nyx

The fires are finally all out. But they left thousands of hectares blackened and twisted and more than half of Tasmania looks like Knocklofty Reserve now. Someone took a continuous drone shot of the whole island from north to south, west to east, hours and hours of footage, and it's like a giant flamethrower was taken to the land. Or like a special Demo-Chem unit came through and took out all the green things and any animals and birds that might have still been living in them, leaving just blackened suggestions of trees and forests behind.

I'm inside again today because of the rain that won't stop. And we're down to our last two packets of rehydro – one for the O'Donnells and one for me and Dad to share – and there's no prospect of any more. The shops don't have any food left in them. We're all downlinking everything we can on how to get Foodaid and Fundaid in our local areas, and people are telling each other on *Freecycle* and *Barteroo* and all these other chat spaces where to find things to eat or drink or sell or buy. But as soon as someone with a good heart lets people know they've got *something* it's already gone in seconds. *First-come-first-served* or *FCFS* is what the message usually says as soon as it's gone up. There's usually a riot if people make it to someone's house to find one hundred other people got there before them and there's nothing to be done about it. People often walk for hours to reach that place, hoping, but there's nothing to show for it in the end except more hunger and maybe serious injury if tempers are up enough. Things have gone way beyond *desperate*.

"These are the end times," Dad will tell anyone in the street who will listen, but no one has time to talk anymore. They are too busy *hanging on*, or boarding up their windows to keep other people out.

The TasPrem's department asked the citizens of Tasmania to uplink to an official announcement at 12 pm today, but it never came. So many people uplinked that maybe the link crashed, or maybe the TasPrem has already fled to the Northland like all the other people still with funds or transpo options, leaving the rest of us here to starve and listen to the endless rain and look at an empty podium on an empty stage that has the TasPrem logo all over it. I almost wish the fires were back, so that at least the world would have some light, heat and color in it. Now it's just always gray, stormy and cold.

"I don't know what we're going to do," I hear Dad tell Mr O'Donnell grimly. "We'll go out again tomorrow and doorknock the area, double-check the servos, supers and megas, but I'm not hopeful."

"Do you …" Mr O'Donnell's voice is tentative, "want us to leave? It may be easier for you and your kid?"

I hear Dad's grunt. "May as well starve here as anywhere, Bruce," he says heavily.

I don't hear Mr O'Donnell's relief, but I can almost feel it through the warped door of my bedroom.

I tell Bea all this. I tell her how we're all trapped here with nothing but one last meal and pots of contaminated rainwater to drink. The desal plant broke down last week from the sheer volume of extra water filling the seas and rivers, so we've got pots and pans outside on the back lawn, collecting all the rainwater we can. It's not brown, but it's filled with grit and tastes ashy and slightly foul. I try not to think about what's in it. Nobody's got any tablets to decontam it with, so we're all just drinking what we collect and hoping that we don't get sick like the Ding family did at number 29. All of them sweating and feverish and weak and laid out in bed, or on the floor where they simply lay down out of exhaustion, for *days*.

I tell Bea now that maybe the time of Dad's flood has finally come and that there's nowhere left to run if the water makes it this far. The old Cat and Fiddle Arcade went under yesterday and people have been fleeing to the inland homes of friends and family that aren't so close to the waterfront. All of us packed tight into this constantly shrinking area.

I hate going outside at the moment, the pounding rain makes it impossible to see where I'm going, or from falling down on the slick ground, but I need to tell Bea how important it is. And I would do that – go outside – only for Bea.

I feel terrible asking for help, I write.

Begging, actually.

If you can do something – not to stop the rain, you can't stop the rain, it's all our vanished Arctic *ice wreaking its final revenge, the Fakenewsmedia says – but something to help <u>us</u>. Invent something, maybe make something? That will create enough food or shelter for us to ride out this terrible rain.*

I'm sure I'm just worrying for nothing, Bea, but this feels different. Deep in my bones, it feels really different. Maybe Dad was right and we should have left while we could have.

I don't know how much longer I'm going to be able to make it back to the Mailbox Tree – I'm running out of paper and it's getting really dangerous to leave home – but I'll keep going until I can't stand up outside anymore.

Nyx

I wait for a break in the rain that doesn't come until it's almost too late to go. Dad's uplinked to his Lady Friend, who's getting impatient and saying it was all a trick that he was coming, all lies to get her to trust him, so he doesn't see me slip out the back door. But Mrs O'Donnell does, the thin, bony baby on her thin, bony hip still crying. Mrs O'Donnell raises a hand, calls out, but I yell, "I'll be back soon! I'll be okay!" and slip and slide, straight for the Mailbox Tree, the note to Bea already wet before my feet hit the edge of the oval that isn't dusty anymore, it's more of a shallow lake now.

I start wading, the water rushing past my shins, toward the base of the giant tree.

Bea

We walk together, up the steep mountainside.

I still can't quite believe I'm here, that *we* are here – that I'd managed to convince almost *everyone* to come with me on this bizarre adventure.

My mom and dad were back there, chatting with my teachers. Groups of my new school friends walk behind me – I am in the lead.

I am their leader.

My brain is having trouble making sense of it all. I was a *nobody*, not so long ago, either ignored or bullied.

I have no idea how any of this is possible. How could the world shift on its axis so completely, in such a short space of time?

Life is change. Life is chaos. Nothing is certain. Nothing ever stays the same.

I don't know if I should forgive them all. I don't know if I can. I only know that, for now, the fate of the world – and Nyx – is more important. She's my best friend. And she is relying on me. I can't let my own small, petty worries get the better of me.

My toe catches on the base of a tree. I hold out my hands to stop my fall. Before I hit the dirt and bark, I jerk – an arm wrapped around me.

I turn to see who caught me. I'm stunned to see it's Sophie – one of the *mean girls gang*. They'd finally caved, and agreed to help, because their refusal was starting to make them look bad and make them unpopular. And that couldn't happen.

"How was your trip?" she asks, mildly, as she helps me back to standing. She raises an eyebrow, eyes sparkling with amusement.

"Fine," I mumble. "Thanks."

I make to walk away, before she can make fun of me anymore.

"Wait!"

I feel a hand on my arm. I don't look, don't want to see or hear what cruel jibe she has in store for me. I just want her to leave me alone, so I can get on with things.

Get on with saving Nyx.

"I'm sorry."

I stop in my tracks. Behind me, I hear fifty pairs of feet standing still as well. Finally, I turn.

Sophie shrugs and rolls her eyes. "I'm sorry," she says, again.

"For … what?" I manage to croak.

"Being a Grade A horror to you," she says. She looks me straight in the eye. She doesn't seem ashamed or embarrassed at all. I marvel at her confidence – to say all this, in front of *everyone*.

A couple of her friends – Maya and Britt – move to join her.

"Yeah," said Maya, her brown eyes huge. "We've been talking about it. We're all sorry."

"We shouldn't have been so horrible," says Britt. "We won't be, again."

Our classmates and teachers watch us, in stony silence. This doesn't feel real. None of it feels real.

"Why?" I whisper.

"Why did we do it?" asks Sophie, catching my meaning. She shrugs. "Because Callie told us to. And to pass the time. Which is the worst excuse *ever*, I know.

To pass the time and ... middle school sucks. If you're not the bully, someone's bullying you. I guess."

It made sense and no sense, all at once.

"Why *me*?" I press.

It's Maya who answers, this time. "Because you're different. And because you're ... kind of a loner. It's easy to bully a kid who's alone."

"We won't do it again," Britt repeats. "You're kind of awesome. This is – kind of – awesome. We understand why you're doing it. If the adults won't do something for the kids of the future – the kids of the present *have* to."

I look behind her, at my classmates. Scan their faces. And I realize. "Callie's not here?"

"She didn't want to come. And we didn't want her to."

I nod. "Okay," I say.

I hear a throat clearing. It's my mom. "You okay, Bea?" she asks, gently.

I nod at her. "I'm okay," I say.

To the mean girls ... to the *girls*, I say, "We need to keep going."

They nod back, smiling. And I don't know if I've forgiven them – don't know if I should. But I know that everything before now is the past. And we're doing this for the future.

And we have to keep going.

Nyx

We haven't eaten for two days.

The O'Donnells started walking yesterday, to go to Republic of Hobart Hospital. Their baby was starting to get malnourished and blue and was crying even more than usual, but weakly. She sounded really different. They said that if they stayed with us for a day longer they were afraid their baby wouldn't make it.

Dad hasn't come out of his bedroom all day because all of our things — all our movecrates — were either stolen or floated off the dock. Everything is gone. When he called to find out where they were the people told him no one had seen them for weeks.

Except for the odd bits we found in a cupboard we forgot to clear, we've got no clothes, no furniture and hardly any money left because Dad's been stood down off work. They don't need council workers at the moment because the council has run out of money and out of projects. His Lady Friend isn't even connecting when Dad uplinks now.

She thinks he was pretending the whole time. And she says she doesn't need two more mouths to feed when she has three of her own at home with nothing to spare.

All I have is Mom's book, her boots and her raincoat, and you can't eat those.

The water is up to our back steps now. If our land didn't slope down the way it does, maybe it would already be inside the house.

Can you do something?

Are you doing anything? I'm sorry to ask. I need to know that you have a plan because we've run out of plans and time.

This may be my last note ever.

The Mailbox Tree is surrounded by water now. It was up to my hips the last time I was there. And there's a current in it, it feels like hands reaching out to pull me down when I wade out, toward the tree.

Bea, I'm so sorry.

I'm so sorry that this is your future. I hope you don't have to see any of this, although I do hope you live a long and happy life with enough to eat and drink all the way through. I hope you have hot and cold days and swimming pools. I hope you have real 'apricot chicken' and 'choco-pudding' and trees. And nice people who don't steal from you because they think you have something they need.

Most of all, I hope that you'll never have to choose whether it's fires or floods that will get you in the end.

If you saw my time, you wouldn't even believe it.

It's not really what you'd call living.

Nyx

Bea

On the mountain, we were making something.

It started with a few posts, hammered into the ground. There were ladies there from the council – engineers – to make sure we did it right. They took measurements and made notes and we had to sign forms and it was all very official and I was sure that one of them – the ladies – would dig the first holes and make the first marks.

But they asked me to.

I have to ask Dad twice to confirm what they meant.

"This is your baby, Bea," he says. "They said that you should do it."

"But I know nothing about how to build a … a … anything," I whisper back, urgently.

Dad laughs. "I know, honey. That's why we're all here for backup."

"I can help." Sophie grins, wide and gentle. "If you want me to. Unless you want to do it yourself …"

I shake my head. "I could use a hand."

Britt raises an arm. "My dad taught me heaps about building," she says. "He … died. But I remember some stuff. Maya and I could help, too, maybe?"

I nod, tears prickling my eyes, and look at my own dad, with gratitude for his … existence. "I'd love it if you'd help too, Dad."

"But you do the first one," Dad insists.

Dad passes me a mallet. "I don't know what to do with it," I insist.

"We'll help you." Mom comes to my side. "You're not alone."

Her best friend, Ali, is there, too. She waves at me. Her fingernails glimmer green and gold in the sunlight.

I look around the assembled crowd. Everyone is watching me. My cheeks warm. I still can't believe they're here. I still can't believe they followed me up here.

Me.

"Thank you," I tell them, in as loud a voice as I can manage. "Thank you for believing me. Thank you for believing in me. And yourselves. The people who come after us will thank us. We won't know it, but when they come here, they'll see what we've done for them and they'll be so *glad*."

"It's completely weird," said Sophie.

"But weird things can be true," said Maya. "My brother is convinced he saw a pixie down the bottom of the garden, once." She raises a shoulder. "Jury's still out on whether he's just a weirdo. After all of this, I think I'd believe anything."

"You're completely weird. But good weird," Britt adds.

"So, you really all do believe in Nyx?" I ask everyone.

"We can see that you do," says Dad. "And we believe in you."

Just then there is a sound behind me – a stick, breaking. It's loud.

I turn.

There's nobody there.

Or, maybe that's not true at all. If time is like a river – she's right here, with us. And everyone else who ever climbed Mount Wellington. In this moment, we're all standing here together in our separate flows of time.

"Do you think that was *her*?" I hear someone whisper.

I turn back around. "I feel like she's here with us," I

tell them. My throat closes over. Tears press at my eyes. "I hope it means that she finds what we're about to build for her."

"We should paint her," Sophie says. "A mural, on the shelter, when we're done. Or is that a dumb idea?"

I make my voice work through the tears. "That's not dumb at all."

Dad pulls me close, in a warm, scratchy woollen hug. "I am so proud of you," he says.

"I still don't know how to do the mallet thingie," I admit, into his shoulder.

"Let me help," he says. "Together, we'll make it look like you know what you're doing. Fake it till you make it."

"I feel like that's what the whole human race is doing, right now," I say.

"There are worse places to start," he says.

For a moment, with my dad's arms around me as we swing the mallet, I forget that we're moving to the mainland soon. In this moment, I feel like Nyx and I are the closest we've ever been.

Nyx

Something makes me sit bolt upright.

It's like I felt a clanging go through my soul. Maybe the sound of a hammer hitting steel. It echoed in my head, waking me up. I look at the falling-apart biosynth band that Mrs O'Donnell left behind by accident in my old bedroom, and it says 1.13am.

I sit up straighter and hug my knees to my chest inside my sleeping bag. It's pouring outside, a steady, roaring stream of water and noise, and the house is dark except for the thin gleam of light coming out from under Dad's bedroom door.

When I fight my way free of my sleeping bag and pad out in my socked feet into the hallway, I can hear him in there, shouting at someone to *Link up, please!*

I creep out toward the back door and slip into Mom's

old ankle boots. They won't keep the rain out for longer than two minutes and will fill up quickly. Especially once I reach the reserve, which is like a lake now. A really scary lake that goes up past my waist these days. One slip and I'll go under and I can't really swim. Swimming lessons stopped so long ago, and before my class really got started, that I can't really swim more than three or four strokes before I start struggling. A muddy, rushing lake that used to be an oval, with its own spooky undercurrent, will be like a death trap.

But something tells me I have to go out to the Mailbox Tree tonight. It might be the last time I ever can.

Things are desperate here. There are no more ships coming to take us up to the Northland – they've suspended the rescue effort. The processing centers there are bursting at the seams and they've told whoever is left in south-eastern Tasmania to move as far inland as we can and just wait things out until *the position is clearer*.

"We'll all die before the position gets any clearer!" Dad had muttered when we'd managed to downlink the latest news bulletin.

Deep in my bones I know that's true. The water's up to our back door now. And no one inland from us needs any more guests – wanted or unwanted. People have started buying guns and covering their gates in planks of wood and surrounding their properties with barbed wire, dogs and sandbags. It will get really ugly when the last bit of food runs out and that's only days away. Dad and I haven't eaten anything for almost four days now. Nothing is growing, nothing is coming in and all we have left is water. Dirty water. And you can't live on that.

I quickly scribble a note to Bea in the dark by the kitchen door. All I have left is the back cover of the last notebook she left me in the tree a few weeks ago. I hope she can see the letters I've gouged into the cardboard in thick capital letters:

I THINK THIS IS THE LAST TIME I CAN GET OUT TO OUR TREE.

IT'S TOO DANGEROUS TO GO OUTSIDE ANYMORE.

THE WATER IS UP TO OUR HOUSE NOW. IT WILL PROBABLY BE INSIDE BY TOMORROW AND WE WILL HAVE TO GO INLAND TO A REFUGEE CENTER. OR TO WHOEVER WILL TAKE US.

THE RESERVE IS A LAKE NOW AND I CAN'T SWIM. NOT REALLY.

WE'VE RUN OUT OF FOOD. PEOPLE ARE STARVING. I HAVE HEARD OF PEOPLE BOILING LEATHER SHOES FOR SOUP AND STRIPPING THE LEAVES FROM PLANTS THEY DON'T KNOW ANYTHING ABOUT.

I JUST WANTED TO SAY GOODBYE.

AND THANK YOU.

FOR THE TREES — AND ALL THE HOPE.

NYX

I have to wipe away a little tear as I write my name with great stabbing strokes.

Then I slip the hard piece of cardboard inside the pocket of Dad's old shirt that I've been using as a nightgown, slip my bare legs into the ankle boots and wade out into the storm.

I don't remember much of the trip there or back.

The rain was so heavy, so angled, that it felt like it was slicing the skin off my face. It just pounded down out of the sky, so hard that it hurt.

I could barely see where I was going and when I reached the reserve the water was up to my rib cage and something hit me so heavily in the ribs – maybe a tree branch or a piece of hard rubbish – that I almost fell beneath the water face-first.

The piece of cardboard was soaked when I slipped it into the knot in the tree.

I couldn't see anything in the darkness beneath the branches, but I could feel that Bea had left me something. A piece of paper wrapped tight around something hard.

Not wanting to lose hold of it I gripped the small package in my teeth as I climbed back down out of the Mailbox Tree. It didn't occur to me until I staggered through the back door at home that I would probably never ever do that again. It was too dangerous to go back out there now, especially if it kept raining like this. Raining like it would never end. Dad hadn't got much right lately except maybe that it was the end of the world.

Dad's light was off now, but the house wasn't silent because the tin roof was hammering from the rain and wind. I stripped off my soaked ankle boots, leaving them to dry by the door. In my bedroom, with freezing, knotty fingers, I turned on my bedside lamp and gently prised open the note.

Something hard fell out. A bright orange boiled candy in a clear plastic wrapper which made my eyes go really wide. I'd only ever read about one of these in vintage books from the turn of the twenty-first century. You used to be able to buy these in things called corner shops, convenience stores and pharmacies. Back when things didn't used to have to be so big, to feed lots of people at once, or to sell big loads of things at once, for efficiency.

I began to read.

Bea

We break for lunch at midday.

"Is an hour okay?" I ask everyone. That's enough time for people to go back down the mountain, if they want to, and eat lunch at home or at one of the South Hobart cafés.

"You want to come with us?" asks Sophie. "We're going to go to Ginger Brown."

"Ali and I are going to grab some stuff from the Salad Bowl, if you want anything," says Mom, looking warily between me and Sophie. She knows that Sophie, Maya and Britt are three of the girls who have been giving me trouble at school since she can remember. I try to communicate with my eyes, to tell her it's okay. But as much as it might be nice to go to Ginger Brown with the girls – to go to a café with *friends*, maybe friends, *almost* friends – I have something more important to do, right now.

I turn to Dad. "Could you take me home, just for the break?" I say. "I have to …" I clear my throat. "Um, I have to visit the Mailbox Tree."

Dad looks confused for a moment – behind him, I can see that Mom and Ali and the girls from school look every bit as befuddled. Then, I see it dawn on Dad first. "You need to send a note to Nyx?" he asks, quietly.

I nod, my cheeks burning.

"That is so cool," says Britt. "Can we come? Can we see?"

There's a fluttering inside me, and a whispering voice, telling me I should not, I should let her come and see the tree. That I would be *cool, wanted, accepted,* if I let her come.

But I shake my head. "Not this time,' I say. "I just … I kind of want to be with Nyx, alone."

I expect Britt to get mad, to cross her arms and pout and say 'whatever' – mutter *freak* beneath her breath.

But she doesn't.

She just says, "Maybe next time?" and smiles and I nod in reply.

Definitely next time.

Back at home, I run to the tree as soon as Dad turns off the car ignition. "I'll make you a sandwich!" he calls out after me.

I climb up the tree, fast as a possum, and I dive my hand into the hole.

I pull out soggy cardboard. I can't believe it's still wet. From rain that's happening seventy years away. In the future.

Oh, no.

I read Nyx's water-smudged note, tears burning at my eyes.

I tear off a piece of paper from the notepad I've taken to carrying around in my pocket and I hastily scribble a note in reply.

It's not there yet — we're still working. At the top of Mount Wellington. But we'll work until it's done. There's a whole team of people from school, engineers from the council, local people who heard and wanted to help. We'll work all the way until nighttime. We'll bury food in big tin chests, deep in the ground. Things that will keep. And things to keep you warm while you wait out your dad's epic flood. There will be enough for you to survive. You will survive, Nyx. And you'll see the structure, no matter how high the water climbs. We're going to paint it, Nyx. We're going to paint it bright and bold. We're going to paint you, so that you will know that we saw you. I saw you. I know I haven't, really, but I imagine you. I see you in my heart and when you know, deep in your gut that there's no time left and you'll have to go — with whoever you can take with you — your safety will be there. I'm going to save you, Nyx. And you're going to save ... I know it might sound mad, but ... I feel like you're with us. It's not there yet, but please hang in there. We may not be able to rebuild your world — but we're going to keep you alive. And then we're going to build more of these places. And we're going to tell everyone we know about what we've done — so that they understand how it important it is. That what we're doing now will keep people, who haven't even been born yet, alive.

As I shove the notepad deeper into my pocket I feel something hard at the bottom of it – a boiled candy from a bag that Britt's mom had handed around to keep us all going. She got the notepaper. Maybe she'll get this. It's the only food I have on me. It's not even food.

I hastily shove the candy into the middle of the note and wrap the paper tight around it. Then I put the tight little package into the hole and clamber back down the tree. I race back to the house. Dad is leaning on the kitchen bench, reading the paper – stories about pandemics and plagues and putrid politicians – and eating a tomato sandwich.

"There's one for you, over—" he begins. I cut him off. We don't have an hour. We don't have any time to waste. Dad's making us leave for the mainland soon so every minute we have left to spend on Mount Wellington, we're going to build and paint and preserve for the future so that it will arrive in Nyx's present.

"Bring it with you," I say. "Bring mine, too. I'll eat in the car. I'm going to find more paint – as much as I can. Meet you at the car in two minutes."

"But you said—"

"I don't care what I said!" I cry, through tears that

won't stop falling. "Nyx needs us *now*, Dad!"

He hesitates for only a moment, a triangle of sandwich halfway to his mouth.

Then he nods and he swallows and he says, "Okay, let's go."

Nyx

I stare hard at the wrapped orange candy in my hand. It looks so shiny and new.

But it was made *decades* before I was born. Can it even be safe to eat?

But I'm so hungry I can feel the saliva just running down my throat as I continue holding it when all I really want to do is to tear the wrapper off and cram it into my mouth.

I'm sorry, Dad, I think guiltily, *but I can't share this one. This is* mine.

I stare at the note with blurry vision, then back at the candy. I haven't had anything to eat all day.

I can't believe Bea is building something … for me. For someone she hasn't even met. And never will. She must have moved to the Northland – what she calls 'the mainland' years before I was born. If she's still alive, she'll be really old. The thought actually makes me shiver.

I can't even conceive of anything being up on kunanyi/ Mount Wellington. The walking track from Knocklofty to the peak is supposed to be haunted. It takes at least two hours to get up there on a cool, clear day – and there haven't been many of those for the past twenty years – and there's no reason to go now when there's no view or birds or greenery anymore. Just blackened earth and rock for miles around. People don't go up there now because everything's blasted or stunted, burned or shriveled, all the way up. Nothing grows up there. And people have heard noises on the track. Like lots of footsteps. The echoes of voices. Some people have even said they've felt things brush past them, or push against them, as if whatever is haunting the track is in a hurry to get somewhere and any living thing that's on the track will only get in their way.

What Bea is asking me to do sounds … crazy. She's asking me, and whoever else is crazy enough to listen to me, to take a huge chance and just climb for hours through heavy rain on stomachs that haven't eaten anything, not properly, for days. No one will believe me.

But they have to, because I believe her. Like the Theater Royal, something's happened up there, something's changed. I have to believe that so that I can convince everyone I can that we need to be brave enough to leave all the things we know about, leave home, and take a chance.

It's not even 4am yet. But as soon as there's any hint of light showing through the curtain of gray rain falling out of the sky I'm going around the street – the whole neighborhood if I have to. If there's food and shelter on Mount Wellington, it's up to me to lead people up there.

Because there's only famine, or worse, where we are.

My gut is screaming at me like it's time to *go*.

I crawl back into my sleeping bag, the hard candy clutched in my hand.

What if it poisons me?

What if no one will listen? Not even Dad, and they stay here and drown in their own houses?

Before I can change my mind, I unwrap the ancient candy that looks brand new in the dim, wavering light of my torch and cram it into my mouth.

I let it dissolve slowly on my tongue for a long time.

It tastes like sunshine.

It tastes like hope.

Or like the past must have tasted.

Or how the future will taste.

I can't wait for the morning to come as the rain beats down and down.

Bea

Burying the food feels like a kind of communion. It feels like giving something to Earth, to the world, to this place, to the *future*.

It feels like we are passing a gift, directly from our hands to the hands of the people who will uncover these packages. It feels like we are, somehow, holding them, nourishing them, making them whole again.

I know everyone else feels it, too. That's why we do it in silence, packing the earth in tight around these giant tin chests that are supposed to withstand the end of the world, a flood to end all floods.

It's not fancy food – it's all in tins or jars and it's dried and cured and preserved with more chemicals than I know how to name. I'm not entirely sure which parts of the animal any of the 'meat' is from, or even if it's really meat at all. It's simple, old-fashioned food, like my grandparents might have eaten, when they were small. It's not fancy quinoa, goji berry, activated almond, green smoothie Instagram kind of food. It's not a time capsule of *now*.

It's food that's only designed to keep them alive long enough to survive the flood and see what's left afterwards.

God, I hope it helps them to survive.

"I feel like we should say a prayer," I whisper. "This feels like a funeral, only … the opposite of a funeral. It's about carrying people to life, not passing them over to death."

Mom takes one of my hands and Dad takes the other and together we begin the 'Our Father' prayer, because it's one that we know everyone else will know, too. All around us, people drop their tools and take each other's hands. It doesn't feel like any of us are strangers, anymore. Not after a day like today.

By the time we finish, there is not one of us dry-eyed.

After the burial of the food, we begin the mural. We pick up brushes and open sample paint tins and one of the older women, with short gray hair, in overalls and sturdy work boots, starts sketching the outline as I tell them what I think Nyx looks like. She stares hard at me for a moment, her head to one side and starts sketching another figure right next to Nyx. Between the two outlines she draws a rainbow. Together, we paint, freehand, inside the woman's sketch. We paint from our hearts.

It takes me a while – absorbed as I am in painting the *Nyx* side of things – to realize that some of the other people are finishing the giant outline of the other person, that's holding Nyx's hand.

When Mom nudges me to take a look, I almost drop my brush.

It's *me*, holding Nyx's hand. The-girl-on-the-wall-me is wearing exactly what I'm wearing today. Down to my striped socks and sneakers.

"Wait, that's not what we–" I begin.

Mom holds a finger up to her lips.

"Just go with it," says Dad.

And so I do.

And at the end of the painting, we add an arrow, pointing down toward where Nyx should dig.

The members of the council who have come plant a sign (I know it's not *really* planting, but it feels like it), that says that anything found buried here is not to be taken – that it is for a girl called Nyx, who will come here in seventy years' time and will need what is buried here to survive a giant flood.

The sign also says that it is against every council bylaw there is, now and into the future, for anyone to take what's here before it's time, and that the council will know who did it – people who come up here are tracked after all – and that *all offenders will be prosecuted.*

"Is that true?" I whisper to Mom.

She lifts a shoulder. "It looks true," she says. "Let's hope it's enough – this sign and the conscience of all the people who come here. Who will tell everyone they know. We'll have to have faith in that."

I nod and I put my head on her shoulder and I say, "We'll have to have faith in humanity."

Nyx

Night and day are the same thing. I only know it's morning after my night of interrupted, uneasy sleep when someone bangs on the front door to let us know the power's completely out – there will be none for days, if not weeks or months – because the wind turbine fields that power West Hobart have been locked down for their own protection and the hydro system has suffered some catastrophic failures overnight.

"A couple of the dams in the Derwent hydropower chain have gone down and it's a mess!" I hear Robert Magee shouting down the hall. "It's back to cave man times, Rich, old boy! Hope you know how to make fire, because I don't, mate."

I drag myself upright, keeping my sleeping bag up around me because the house is icy. The air is as warm as the rain outside, the only difference being that we're mostly dry.

I find Dad still standing in the hall staring vacantly at the closed door long after Mr Magee has gone. "It's all gone to pot," he mutters. I can barely hear him over the rain.

"Dad?" I say.

He doesn't turn. His shoulders are slumped, the same way they stayed for months after Mom died and before he found his Lady Friend – who doesn't want him anymore.

"Dad!" I shout, a bit frightened now.

He doesn't turn for a long time. "What?" he says, still not looking at me.

"We've got to go," I say, shuffling closer.

He gives a laugh without an ounce of joy in it. "Go where?" he says numbly, his eyes red-rimmed from lack of sleep or worse. "Nowhere to go and nothing to bring there anyway. We've lost it all. Everything we have in the world is in this house, Nyxie."

He focuses on me with difficulty. "In this house that we're about to lose to the rain. I'm going to have to take apart the walls of this place just to keep us warm. If there's even a dry place left in it to light a fire on."

I gasp and hug my sleeping bag closer around me as Dad slumps to the ground, sitting with his head in his hands at my feet, his elbows resting on his knees. "We're trapped, Nyx. There's no money and no food, and soon there will be no air. I've failed you. The flood's here. It's over. And I wasn't ready. No Plan A—" he gives a harsh laugh and I know he's thinking about his vanished life on the Northland, "and no Plan B."

Dad and I haven't seen eye to eye since Mom died, but I don't hesitate. I crouch down beside him and shake him by the forearms. He's still covering his face, just overcome with despair.

"I've got a Plan B," I say firmly.

Dad shakes his head and moans into his hands and I shout it just to wake him up out of his hopeless trance. "I've got a Plan B, it's up on Mount Wellington. You know, kunanyi." I point up and away behind us.

Dad looks up through his fingers at me. "There's nothing up on Mount Wellington. The bushfires and illegal chemdumping took out everything on the mountain. We'd still just die up there, even if it took a few more days for the water to reach us. It's a wasteland on top of the Mount. We'll survive just long enough to starve to death if we go up there."

I shake my head, my entire heart in my eyes. "There's this girl called Bea," I tell him, sitting down on the floor in front of my Dad. "And I need you to really listen to me now because I think that while we've been down here, slowly drowning, she's been building our Plan B for us, up there."

"*How–*" Dad tries to interrupt, but I reach one hand tentatively out of my sleeping bag and grip him by the wrist, and I start telling him about the Mailbox Tree and everything that's happened since I left that note written on a torn page of Mom's old book inside the knot in its trunk.

Bea

We packed up slowly. I got the feeling that nobody wanted to leave.

It felt like we were doing something important here. None of us wanted to go back to ... life.

I, especially, did not want to go back to life as it had been, *before*.

Before, when school was frightening, and leaving this place even more so. I felt even more connected to this land, now and, for the first time, I felt connected to some of the people from my school. Everything was beginning to weave together and the tapestry of all of it looked so beautiful to me.

But was it only the spell of this place and what we were doing, and Nyx and the Mailbox Tree? When I walked away from here, would the tapestry turn to dust?

I felt a hand in mine.

Mom.

"You look sad," she said. "I thought you would be happy. We've done such an amazing thing, here – *beyond* amazing. We can do it again. We'll do *more*."

I took a deep breath. "I don't want to leave," I said. I had said it so many times. But this time felt bigger, brighter, more burning and brilliant and I felt like Mom could see it.

She nodded. "Maybe ... we can figure something out," she said. "If it's so important to you. I feel like ... I have learned today that this–" She gestured to me and to Dad, who was putting up a sign, and to the forest as a whole, to all of our city down below. "This is what's most important. Time and life is short and I think ..." She smiled, blinking at glimmering tears. "I think I want to stay, too. So we'll figure something out, okay?"

I nodded. It was all I could do, tears of my own tumbling from my lashes and disappearing on the forest floor.

I felt another presence at my side. Three of them. Sophie, Maya and Britt.

"We thought we'd go for ice cream at the docks,"

Sophie said, smiling. "You want to come?"

I smiled back at her, but I shook my head. "Next time," I said. "I just want to stay here a while – just a little while. With Mom and Dad." I looked up at the trees. *And Nyx,* I added, silently.

Sophie nodded. "Next time, definitely," she said. She leaned a little closer. "Things are going to be different now," she said. "I promise."

She pulled me into a hug and let go, and then Maya and Britt walked away, toward their own families.

And I let Mom hold me again. I sank into her. I leaned into her shoulder and breathed her in and I breathed in the scent of the forest and I breathed in all the good things and let the bad things go.

And above me, a kookaburra began to laugh. And I laughed with it – with tiredness and relief and joy and all of it.

And I felt, as I did it, another arm around me. Strong and stable and full of so much love. Holding me up.

I turned to my side.

There was nobody there.

But there was, of course.

I knew there was.

And she would be there always.

And anything I did, from now on, I'd be doing for people like her. For the world she'll live in.

Nyx

We set out – me, Dad, the Dings (all five of them, although they were still sick and weak from the poisoned water), only three of the four Magees because the oldest son, Rhys, refused to leave home, the three Ismails and two Bryants (a young married couple with serious faces) from Warwick Street and an elderly couple with heavy accents whose names I didn't catch from Lansdowne Crescent. Fifteen people out of all the frantic doorknocking that Dad and I did after I told him the story of Bea and me. The Schustermans wouldn't even open the door to us, even though we've known them since practically the second I was born.

Dad hadn't believed me straightaway, he'd argued and raged and huffed, but when I showed him what was left of the 'Neverending Story' notebook and the clear plastic wrapper that had held the candy that tasted like sunshine and hope, all of Bea's notes – I let him read every single one in order – something in his face changed. He looked like *Dad*. The way he used to look. A *take charge* kind of person. Not completely defeated by life.

"I haven't seen a wrapper like that in *years*," he had whispered. He'd even held it up to his nose for a sniff.

He'd told me to wear everything we had left between us, me in Mom's old ankle boots stuffed with socks, my own change of clothes and Mom's old raincoat and him in an old coat that had belonged to his granddad that Dad hadn't thought fit to pack for the cargo so it was luckily still in the house. We raced up and down the street, knocking on every door. And when most of the people we'd known for most of my life shook their heads or refused to even hear what we had to say, we ran up and down Warwick Street and Lansdowne Crescent, too, (well, the bit closest to us anyway because we were tired by then) and told whoever would listen the story until our mouths were dry.

Fifteen people, other than me and Dad, were all the people who believed us, and said they would come. By midday – although you couldn't really tell it apart from any other hour of the day because the sky was the color of midnight and the wind was howling and rattling all the windows and the rain was driving straight into our faces, they'd all gathered on our front porch. Some of them carried two bags of things each, especially the old people from Lansdowne Crescent whose names I wouldn't learn now until we reached the top; if we reached it at all. And I worried that the bags would be too heavy or that, by the time we got there (if we got there), everything inside would be ruined. Dad had nothing in his hands but a wind-up torch from the olden days, a pocketknife and an old firelighter which barely sparked, and I had Mom's book in my inside raincoat pocket and that was all.

We all wore hats and mismatched coats and the heaviest shoes we could find and the moment we set foot, together, off our front porch we were already drenched and freezing. Immediately behind me, the Dings made sounds of distress through their teeth, staggering sideways in the storm because they were so thin and weak from not having kept anything down for a long time. The Magees actually broke down in tears outside their house and Mr Magee had to stop Mrs Magee from running straight back inside to her oldest child, Rhys, who was looking at us through the front window with haunted eyes. The Bryants and Ismails had to help the old people or take their bags before we even got further than the end of Blackwood Avenue. Dad shot me a look under the hood of his ancient coat, just once, as we turned into Lansdowne Crescent and made for Knocklofty Terrace, and it felt like we would all retreat and scatter back indoors before we even really began walking.

But I led them on, retracing my steps toward Knocklofty Reserve exactly the same way I'd taken to reach the lookout that night and retrieve the rusty locket, the top of my head pointing straight into the storm that was blowing into all our faces. Occasionally, Dad would tug at the end of my raincoat to tell me to stop and wait because we'd lost sight of someone, or someone needed a rest, badly. None of us could even talk to each other because it felt like we were moving through a hurricane, or the inside of a vast, dark, wild beast that was bucking and rearing and never still.

Before we'd locked up our house for maybe the last time, checking to make sure we'd closed up everything we could close and left everything as tidy as possible in case we ever managed to get back, Dad and I had talked about how, when he was a little boy, his granddad had taken him on the walk up kunanyi.

"The frog ponds were still there, then," Dad had said, "although the actual frogs were all dead at that stage and the "water" had been infested with this colorful algae that looked like poison. And the smell! Goodness. Safe to say, Granddad and I never walked the Summit Loop together again. By the time we got back from the mount we were in all kinds of trouble with my mom, my dad, my granny, all of them saying it was haunted, it was a bad place, and forbidding us ever to go back. But Granddad had made it seem like an adventure, Nyx." Dad's eyes had been sad. "Granddad remembered it when it was all green and alive and when we were walking, and he was telling me where all his favorite spots had been, I could almost see it – being green and alive. It's hard to explain. But I would like to see it again. Even if it *is* the last place I ever see."

Before we'd set out, Dad had told me that there were all these tracks in the olden days, that crisscrossed with each other. They had names like Organ Pipes and Fern Tree, Radford, Panorama and Zig-Zag. He'd told me not to head all the way toward the lookout, like last time, but to take the Zig-Zag track because it was the most direct way to the top. "But it's going to be tough, Nyx," Dad had warned. "And we may have old people with us, which is going to make it tougher – a lot tougher."

Dad had been right. It was harder than anything I could have imagined and all of my life spent downlinking and uplinking in my tiny bedroom in West Hobart had not prepared me for any of it.

The climb seemed to take a thousand years, through the blackened stumps of ancient ferns and blasted trees. We fell up crooked walkways, skinning our hands and knees on things that might once have been rock steps, or old walking tracks. The old signposts we came across infrequently were blank because the words had long since burned or rotted away. Riverbeds that had once been dry were like torrents or waterfalls, and one of the old people lost a precious bag of things when they stumbled across a buried log and the handles of their worn-out sports bag were pulled out of their hands by the white-capped current. Some of the paths were lined with ghostly, densely packed fingers – the remnants of dead trees in vast numbers. Once I looked up through half-closed eyes, my frozen fingers jammed into the depths of my armpits, and I swear I thought I saw giant's teeth looming in the distance, briefly glimpsed between jagged spears of lightning.

The trail got thinner and thinner, more rocky. Our group began to spread out, like a long, straggly string, but I couldn't stop moving upward and forward, because if I did, I would never start again. I'd never been so cold or tired or afraid in my entire life. The rain would not stop, it would not stop, and I screamed at one point as I lost my footing on some loose shale and slid down the slope on my front for at least ten precious feet. Dad had to clamber down and pull me upright, shouting in my face to *Keep going!* as he looked back below us on the track and counted the heads of everyone struggling up behind us.

My entire world was rushing rain, slippery boulders, mud and fallen trees as big as mythical dinosaurs that had somehow laid down and died, right in my path. Then my feet hit something that felt like … a road. A real road – like the ones we'd all left behind.

"Dad!" I screamed in excitement.

Behind me, quite a long way, Dad nodded in understanding, his face lighting up inside his tightly bound hood.

If I could have run, I would have. Scrambling up fallen rocks on hands and knees at one point I broke out onto – the summit. The winds were so strong up here that it felt like, if I took a step too quickly, I might fly right off the top of the mountain. Like one of those eagles I'd seen once in a downlinked video at school.

Through hooded eyes I scanned the summit. I was standing in the remains of an old blacktop carpark for Autos and in the distance stood an old concrete and stone building that faced down onto Hobart below, now missing its roof and windows. Just this oddly-shaped thing that kind of reminded me of a jaw filled with broken teeth, or a worn-out shoe turned upside down. But there was nothing near me that looked remotely like something built by just one girl and her friends, and I wanted to howl. Whatever Bea had prepared for us couldn't have lasted through all the years and weather between us. There was nothing near the broken old lookout building except busted old wooden walkways that fell down between jagged fingers of stone.

Screaming winds, spear-like rain and icy air. I spun on the spot and that's all I could see, hear, feel.

Dad had been right. Maybe we'd last a few more days

than we would have down there. But we had nothing to shelter in up here and nothing to eat. People are pretty simply really, at the heart of everything. Food, water, shelter, love. That's really all we need. And we didn't have two of those four things up here, on kunanyi. Too much water, yeah. But maybe we wouldn't even have love, once all of them saw what I saw.

When Dad reached me, his face was grim. "I've *killed* us!" I screamed into his face in despair. "There's nothing here but rocks, Dad, *rocks!*"

I flung a hand out at the shadowy group of standing stones below the busted lookout and wept into the front of Dad's ancient coat as the wind howled and we both shook from cold and hunger. One by one, the others struggled up to where we were standing and I was too scared to look into any of their faces because I didn't want to see the heartbreak there.

We were all silent as we finally gathered together and stared at the roofless lookout. "Is that where …?" Mr Ding shouted with a look of anguish on his exhausted, hunger-ravaged features. The old people were helped to a seat on our small pile of our belongings as Dad walked forward, toward the broken lookout, his shoulders slumped. Then I saw his figure suddenly stiffen and his arms began to wave and windmill from where he was standing across the ruins of the old carpark.

I lumbered over to him through the driving wet. "There's something down there, near where the ... oh, what had Granddad called it? Boardwalk? Near where the 'boardwalk' used to end!" he shouted. "There's something that isn't rocks or grass. Can you see it?"

I was shaking my head even as lightning split the sky from end to end and I saw a flash of corrugated metal. A low structure, built up against one side of the boardwalk and made out of wood that was bleached gray with age. It was easy to miss because it wasn't hugging the dangerous side – the side that fell down into sheer space – but the inward side of the boardwalk. In fine weather it would be pretty hard to spot, but in storm conditions like these, the structure was almost invisible.

I stumbled across to our small, exhausted party and one by one we helped each other up and shouldered people's bags – it didn't matter whose they were – and picked our way carefully down beside the remains of the treacherous wooden boardwalk that had once allowed kids like my dad to look at the view. For a moment, I paused to take in a view of Hobart that literally took my breath away. From here, up high, it still looked beautiful – not like a place that was slowly drowning. I almost imagined that I could see the giant canopy of the Mailbox Tree towering above the homes we'd all left behind.

We all began to lurch and stumble when we finally saw the building for what it was – a sturdy, but small, hut made of tin and iron, stone and wood. I screamed into the wind and charged forward, faster than all of them.

Clenching my fists in victory above my head, I waited until all seventeen of us reached the door. The hut wasn't much taller than my dad, with a shallowly-pitched tin and iron roof that looked like it had been welded and bolted out of different types and pieces of metal, but it looked whole. The walls and roof of the building appeared to have no holes in them. We had *shelter*.

Bea had done it. She'd built something in her present that had lasted into my future.

There was just a simple iron bolt on the peeling iron and wood door that might once have been painted green. The others crowded around me and Dad eagerly. Standing outside that hut, below the level of the broken boardwalk, it felt almost warm suddenly; the rain almost bearable.

Dad and I looked at each other apprehensively as we stood with our hands on the bolt. *What if it was rusted shut?* Our eyes said. *What if, even if we get this thing open, there's nothing there?*

Dad cranked the handle on his olden days torch a few times then turned it on as I pulled back on the bolt; helped by at least two other people to move the old protesting thing in its rusty channel.

Holding the weak torch beam up high, Dad jammed the door open with his body as we all crowded inside out of the rain.

It sounded like a battle was going on outside as we huddled together inside that snug little building. The rain falling on the metal roof sounded like a hail of falling stones. But we didn't mind that at all because what we saw almost stopped our hearts – a time and weather-faded picture of two girls, holding hands. Faint, but still pretty, surrounded by painted wildflowers with a rainbow arcing between them. Dad read the words off the sign fixed below the rainbow in wonder. "It says there will be other places like this one day, all over the island. And it's you, love," he shouted. "You and Bea in that picture! The sign is telling us – actually it's telling *you*, and only you – to dig here, right *here*."

Young Mr Bryant's eyes widened and he threw his backpack off his shoulders throwing everything inside out of it until he found what he was looking for. "I figured that, after the flood, we'd need to plant things to eat. To start again," he said shyly, over the sound of rain hitting the sheet metal roof above us. "Jenna said I was crazy."

Young Mrs Bryant – Jenna – rolled her eyes but they were smiling.

Mr Bryant held up a rusty old hand trowel. Crowding around him, we all watched as he started to dig at the feet of the painted girls. One brown, one pale. At my feet, and Bea's.

"Thank you," I whispered. Around me, the others did the same, to the sound of rain falling like hail stones, to the sound of digging.

AUTHORS' NOTE

Thank you for picking up this book. We hope that it made you think about the incredible world we live in, just a smidge more. We're hoping that the day where all the ancient forests are gone, the seas turn to acid, and birds, bats and snakes have almost entirely disappeared is just – fiction. Cli-Fi. Not real in the slightest.

We're a little like Bea and Nyx – we've never met in real life, and have used an electronic kind of Mailbox Tree to write the very book you're holding in your hands; dropping chapters to each other like notes into the knot of a giant tree.

One of us lives in Tasmania – just like Nyx does – and one of us lives in "the Northland", the mainland, that Bea and Nyx were afraid of moving to. But luckily for us, we may one day get to meet each other in real life, and walk into the Theater Royal in Hobart, together, to look at the beautiful lights. We don't need to bury something in the ground, or to plant trees, for the other to find – years into the future – because we're not separated by time. And we're lucky, just like you are, because we're living in an age that is still green and alive; where we can still do things to help ourselves, our communities, and our world, stay that way for, hopefully, a lot longer.

When people think about climate change – long-term shifts in temperature and weather that can have stark consequences for food and water security and health and safety, particularly for the most vulnerable people in the world, including children – it feels enormous. It feels impossible, almost like looking up the face of Mount Everest and thinking – How do I conquer that? What can one person really do?

One person can do a lot.

For instance, one person can choose to turn off the lights (when they don't need them); to wear an extra jumper rather than turn the heater up another three degrees; to eat more locally and sustainably (maybe even grow your own!); to make better travel choices (including using your feet, where possible!); to plant more trees or advocate for more green spaces; to not litter; to repair, reuse and recycle (e.g. because fast fashion harms the environment and the vulnerable people who are forced, by their circumstances, to make it); to adopt and love an abandoned animal (we've done that, and it's enriched our lives beyond measure); and to be kinder to the people around you because they may not be experiencing the kind of life you're living.

One person can do a lot.

Add all those singular people together? And you've got a vast crowd that can start helping to dial our collective greenhouse gas emissions down, and turn this big ship we're all sailing on at almost 1,500 miles per hour – Mother Earth – around. We'll all be able to really breathe again. To walk more lightly and treat all our fellow travelers – including every plant, bug, bird, animal and invertebrate – with more care.

The Mailbox Tree is us, in a very small, quiet way, trying to show you how important and unique and powerful you are. You can do something. And in doing something, you're going to find there's a community of people out there, doing their somethings as well to try to reverse climate change for the generations that will come after all of us.

You can be a force for change like Bea is, so that Nyx's future – like the futures of the kids that come after you – is something different, something better.

Thank you for picking up this book. Thank you for doing something today, no matter how tiny, to help all of us.

ABOUT THE AUTHORS

Rebecca Lim is an award-winning writer, illustrator and editor and the author of over twenty books, including *Tiger Daughter* (a CBCA Book of the Year and Victorian Premier's Literary Award-winner), *The Astrologer's Daughter* (A Kirkus Best Book and CBCA Notable Book) and the bestselling *Mercy*. Her work has been shortlisted for the Prime Minister's Literary Awards, NSW Premier's Literary Awards, Queensland Literary Awards, the Margaret and Colin Roderick Literary Award and Foreword INDIES Book of the Year Awards, shortlisted multiple times for the Aurealis Awards and Davitt Awards, and longlisted for the Gold Inky Award and the David Gemmell Legend Award. She is a co-founder of Voices from the Intersection and co-editor of *Meet Me at the Intersection*, a groundbreaking anthology of YA #OwnVoice memoir, poetry and fiction.

Kate Gordon grew up in a very bookish house, in a small town by the sea in Tasmania. After studying performing arts and realizing she was a terrible actor, Kate decided to become a librarian. She never stopped writing and, in 2009, she applied for and won a Varuna fellowship, which led to all sorts of lovely writer things happening. Kate's first book, *Three Things About Daisy Blue*, was published in 2010. Her most recent publications are the middle-grade novels in the 'Direleafe Hall' series, and *Aster's Good, Right Things*, which won the CBCA Book of the Year for Younger Readers.